*The
Imagination
of the Heart*

~~walking~~ ~~Living~~ The Imagination of the Heart

(1) My ~~land~~ As Mama used to say tomo~~
will be my 80th birthday. ~~It's~~ almost eighteen year
Sailor was ~~asked to katrina~~ killed in a c
~~and I still cant believe it~~ ~~Anyway~~ now I walk in
imagination of my heart as spake Jerem
~~the only way to keep Sailor alive~~ might
take the time I have left to ~~tell~~ ~~my only~~
set down best I can my last thoughts
I'm able. Only one interested probably
be ~~my~~ Sailors and my one and only dhu~~
~~son~~ Pace Roscoe Ripley. Pace is 58 har
believe. These days Pace is in N.O. rebu~~
that city after Hurricane Katrina totalled
He got himself a little construction comp~~
~~out~~ to Metairie so I don't see him much as I'd.
~~Not~~ too long after Sailor~~ passed I m~~
from New Orleans back to my home place
Bay St Clement ~~in~~ north Carolina to li~~
Mamas closest and dearest friend Dolce
Delahoussaye in her big old house ha~~
nobody in it but her. ~~After so I~~
~~Br~~ We got along just great for about ten
then at 92 she ~~broke her hip~~ fell off a
stool peeling an apple, broke her hip and had to ~~stay~~
the Hattie McDaniel Home for Women of a Cer~~

The Imagination of the Heart

BOOK SEVEN OF
THE STORY OF SAILOR & LULA

BARRY GIFFORD

SEVEN STORIES PRESS
New York ❋ Toronto ❋ London ❋ Melbourne

A Seven Stories Press First Edition

Seven Stories Press
140 Watts Street
New York, NY 10013
www.sevenstories.com

In Canada: Publishers Group Canada, 559 College Street, Suite 402, Toronto, ON M6G 1A9

In the UK: Turnaround Publisher Services Ltd., Unit 3, Olympia Trading Estate, Coburg Road, Wood Green, London N22 6TZ

In Australia: Palgrave Macmillan, 15–19 Claremont Street, South Yarra, VIC 3141

College professors may order examination copies of Seven Stories Press titles for a free six-month trial period. To order, visit http://www.sevenstories.com/textbook or send a fax on school letterhead to (212) 226-1411.

An excerpt from an in-progress version of this book appeared in the magazine *First Intensity* (Lawrence, Kansas).

Book design by Jon Gilbert

Library of Congress Cataloging-in-Publication Data

Gifford, Barry, 1946-
  The imagination of the heart / Barry Gifford. -- 1st ed.
    p. cm. -- (The story of Sailor and Lula ; bk. 7)
  ISBN 978-1-58322-873-9
  1. Older women--Fiction 2. North Carolina--Fiction. 3. Man-woman relationships--
Fiction I. Title.
  PS3557.I283I43 2009
  813'.54--dc22

                                          2008038725

Printed in the USA

9 8 7 6 5 4 3 2 1

To the memory of Marshall Clements

"At the end of what is
necessary, I have come
to a place where there
is no road."

—IRIS MURDOCH

*   *   *

"I ain't goin' nowhere.
I been where I'm goin'."

—AMOS MILBURN

I

My land as Mama used to say tomorrow will be my 80th birthday. Its almost eighteen years since Sailor was killed in a car wreck when that dumb boy in a Apache pickup cut in front of him from the shoulder of the road as Sail was headed on to the Huey P. Long Bridge. All these years and I still cant believe it. Now I walk in the imagination of my heart as spake Jeremiah. Might as well take the time I have left to me on the planet to set down best I can my last thoughts while Im able. Only one interested probably will be Sailors and my one and only child our son Pace Roscoe Ripley. Pace is 58 hard to believe. These days Pace is in NO rebuilding that city after Hurricane Katrina near about totaled it. He got himself a little construction outfit over in Metairie so I dont see him much as Id like. Not too long after Sailor passed I moved from New Orleans back to my home place of Bay St. Clement North Carolina to live with Mamas closest and dearest friend Dalceda Delahoussaye in her big old house had nobody in it but her. We got along great for about ten years then at 92 she fell off a kitchen stool while she was peeling an apple broke her hip and had to stay at the Hattie McDaniel Home for Women of a Certain Age. Dal lasted close on a year there before the Lord called her. I wonder did He hear her last words to me Lula there aint no beast so fierce as a proven woman. I been puzzling over this since Dal said it and I dont guess I got it figured out yet what she exactly meant. Oh well it wont be so very long before Ill get to ask her in person.

2

I will speak that I may be refreshed says Job. I suppose thats why Im writing now. Actually I always been interested in language or languages I should say. I looked it up in Paces old high school encyclopedia and found out there been nine chief language families in the history of the world. They are African Semitic Indo-European or Aryan Indo-Chinese Japanese Ural Austronesian North American Indian and South American Indian. Of course these are divided into many smaller groups the Semitic for instance has Phoenician Hebrew Arabic Aramaic and Ethiopic all languages of the Holy Bible. Im sure in the translating a lot was lost or changed which could be one good reason why so many people take Gods word different. I am only astonished that more than two persons at all get along anywhere any more it sure seems like they mostly dont. For my 80th I stayed in the house and didnt answer the telephone which rang once early in the morning and again late in the afternoon. I figure it was Pace calling from New Orleans but I just didnt feel like talking. Ill call him and tell him I survived thats if I do of course. I hate to say it but if it aint Sailor on the other end of the line I dont care if Im on it or not. I remember when he used to call me from prison after we got off Id cry like there was no tomorrow and now there really aint.

3

Soon after I left NO to live with Dal in Bay St. Clement
I drove over to the spot where Sailor and I first declared to
one another our absolute undying love. I parked my 1989
Mercury Nightcat next to the Cape Fear light house and
took a walk. Just a closer walk with thee I was thinking thee
being my own gone gone gone Sailor Ripley. It was in the
Cape Fear Hotel that we had reconsummated our love once
again after hed been released from the Pee Dee Correctional
Facility following the incident resulted in the death of one
Bob Ray Lemon. Sailor had only been defending my honor
he never was nothing but correct so far as I was concerned
so depositing him in Pee Dee was a waste of our time and
the resources of the state of North Carolina being as there
was nothing in him to correct in the first place. I was sad to
see the old Cape Fear Hotel had been closed down. An eld-
erly lady pruning her 'Bama Boy roses across the road told

me it happened a couple or more years before things around there were sure more quiet now. I went around back of the hotel to the porch Sail and I sat out on watching the river flow into the Atlantic Ocean as I stood there the tears didnt stop for the longest time. Later I told Dal Id gone there she said honey your mama Marietta thought suffering kept a person from forming too pretty an opinion of their self is how she put it. Nobodys so special the Good Lord dont make them suffer some. How else the heart gets tough enough it dont break completely Dal said otherwise there wouldnt be one person left standing on the planet.

4

Last night I had a dream I was with some people coming from a party in the Quarter walking down Ursulines toward Decatur and here come Sailor in a white Cadillac convertible sitting next to some little blonde driving with the top down looked like Meg Ryan. He had all his hair so it was Sail in his younger days I dont know how old I was. Sailor and the girl sped on by some of us shouted Hey Sailor but he didnt notice or hear. I could hear music blasting from the Cadillac I didnt recognize classical Mozart or something. Must have been what she liked since I never knew Sailor Ripley to listen to anything other than rock or R and B. Thunder and lightning struck just then and rain started coming down hard. It was night but the sky was all lit up with zig zag streaks like vapor trails from jet planes and suddenly they formed together to spell out the words And the children of Israel did evil again in the sight of the Lord. I woke up wet with sweat and called for Dal but then realized she was gone too. I got up and drank half a can of cold Ginger Ale it calmed me down. I went back to bed and read in an old paperback mystery Dal had called The Sailors Rendezvous isnt that strange. Takes place in France.

5

Beanys coming for a visit. Its been nearly 20 years since we actually set blue eyes on one another and being she and I been considering each other best friends for three times that long its a scandal. Beany Thorn never was no favorite of Mamas thats for sure on account of Beanys being so wild and more than most unpredictable. She married first to a man named Elmo Pleasant had a couple kids with him while at the same time he was knocking up highschool girls all over the states of Louisiana and Texas. She tossed his ass out for good just before Sailor got out of jail the first time. Beanys been living in Plain Dealing with her daughter Hedy Lamarr Music and her husband Delivery and their oldest boy Melton who Beany says aint never going to leave home it looks like hes 37 years old. Delivery hes a midget and so is Melton. Delivery and Hedy Lamarrs two other children Spike Jones and Tizane Naureen are normal persons and live in Baton Rouge. Beany says Delivery is a good man and good husband to her daughter who owns a produce stand up on the state highway. There was a time Beany got committed to the nut house at Oriental this was just before her divorce from Elmo. I visited her there and she was so furious at Elmo who had got his lawyer cousin Arafat De Forest the one later got sent up for having sexually molested his own son to file charges Beany abandoned their children for days at a time while she was taking pills that deranged her mind. It was all I could do in my power to keep her from sticking an icepick up Elmos right nostril to disable his motor ability while he was asleep after she got out. Beany got full custody of their kids despite her stretch at Oriental after she proved beyond a doubt Elmo had fathered at least two children by underage girls out of wedlock. Thats a terrible word I think wedlock makes marriage sound like a prison which it is I guess for some though was not for me and my Sailor. Beany arrives tomorrow on the three oclock train and I cant hardly wait.

6

"*Hey*, darlin', is that you?"

"What's become of me is what this is."

"Stop it, Lula, you look terrific. It's me who's gone from bein' Miss Grape to Miss Raisin. Let me see if you still got a butt."

Beany Thorn took hold of Lula and turned her around.

"Don't that beat hell, honey, you do!"

Lula giggled. "Hush, Beany, people'll hear."

"Girl, they ought to see! You'd win the Miss Octogenarian of North Carolina contest, if they had one. Do they?"

"Stop it, baby, I'm awful glad to see you, too."

The two women hugged. Beany Thorn picked up her one little fake alligator bag that her daddy, Deacon Don Thorn, had given her on her seventeenth birthday, two days before she'd been packed off to Oriental the first time.

As they began walking away from the train platform, Lula asked, "That all you brought?"

"For a person who might not make it past today, it's enough. As Saint Scarlett O'Hara said, 'Tomorrow is another day, so let's worry about it when and if it gets here.'"

Once they were settled in wicker rockers on the wrap-around porch of Dal's house—Lula insisted on calling it that even after Mrs. Delahoussaye's passing—each with a chimney in hand filled with crushed ice, Bombay gin and a teaspoonful of sugar, the two lifelong friends appraised one another more carefully.

"Take a sip, Beany, it'll cool you down."

Beany did, then said, "Lula, you're really more than a friend deserves—you remembered my fondness for Bombay."

"Bought a bottle just because you were comin', though I have to say I don't mind it myself."

"Happy days!" declared Beany, holding up her glass.

"Happy days!" Lula repeated.

"Look at us, Lula, two old biddies no use to nobody."

"At least we ain't pollutin' the planet. Not too much, anyway. We don't drive SUVs or use tampons."

"Lula, you ever think about sex?"

"My land, Beany! Thank the Good Lord, no."

"I must confess, sweetie, I do. Not that I want it, necessarily. After all, I'm dry as a bone. But the thought of havin' a man's big old hairy arms around me comes on now and again. I even have orgasms in my dreams."

Lula gagged on a large swallow of ice cold gin.

"Beany, after all these years you still terrify me."

"Saw a young man in the Wal-Mart the other day—Tuesday, I guess it was—wearin' a sweatstained wifebeater made me tremble. I swear I coulda sucked on him like a Holloway All-Day. Don't tell me you don't have them thoughts even once in a while."

"Beany, I don't want to talk about it. No, in fact. I told you."

Beany ran her tongue over her lips, savoring the flavor of the Bombay gin and sugar, and said, "I got to keep alive in my mind the possibility that I got at least one more romantic episode comin' my way."

"I heard the most terrible thing on the radio last night," said Lula. "You know I can't sleep more than three or four hours, so I listen to the radio in the night."

"I ain't slept more than four hours at a crack since I was twelve, Lula. Ever since I figured out I'd be takin' the Big Dirt Nap someday. Didn't want to miss nothin' before then."

"Heard that the French fella was always explorin' the waters of the world—can't recall his name, somethin' like

Crusoe only his first name weren't Robinson, he's dead now—was in a submarine at the bottom of Lake Tahoe in California, and discovered the bodies of a hundred or more Chinese men frozen intact. Turns out these men had been workin' a job out there in about the year 1900 and thought they were bein' taken to the other side of the lake after their job was finished."

"Did the boat go down in a storm?"

"Uh uh. The terrible part is that the bosses didn't want to pay 'em, so they clubbed all them poor little Chinese men and boys and threw their bodies overboard. The lake is super deep and frozen at the bottom, which is why the corpses is all preserved."

"Did the French guy fish out the bodies?"

"Crusoe said it was too horrible and people couldn't deal with it, so he left 'em there. Ain't that the most horrifyin' thing?"

Beany nodded and drank down the contents of her glass.

"Sounds like somethin' Elmo's partner Emilio Zarzoso mighta done. Remember him, Lula? The one who did twenty years for murderin' his wife with a poisonous viper he claimed was an exotic pet escaped from its cage?"

Lula finished off her drink and said, "Time for another sugar gin, Beany, don't you think?"

7

Beanys visit is raising my spirits at least I feel like I got more pep. Theres a word hardly heard much any more. Beany is always agitating about something now its our going off together on a oceanliner cruise to meet rich widowers. I asked her what on earth they would want with us old women and she answered me companionship. These are men cant do for themselves and get lonely not having anything much to do since they retired. They need a woman to get their motor started again. I cant get my own motor started most days so how Im supposed to get him going? Told Beany Id think on it but it seems to me theres a whole lot more widows around than widowers and a man like that needs a young woman to start him up. Beany she wont take no easy so best for me to do is just humor her. Middle of last night I heard noise in the kitchen so I got up went in and theres Beany hitting the gin this time cut with orange juice. She looked at me and said Terrors are turned upon me they pursue my soul as the wind. I recalled from my time with the Church of Reason Redemption and Resistance to Gods Detractors to say My bones are pierced in me in the night season and my sinews take no rest. Beany smiled a good smile she still got almost all her own teeth left and said I know baby I couldnt sleep neither.

8

Beany and Lula were seated outside in the garden of the Lion's Mouth Cafe fingerdipping sardines and Saltines in red salsa and drinking Cosmopolitans. The sun was just about down for the day.

"How you like that Cosmo?" asked Beany. "It's what the twenty and thirty somethin's prefer these days."

Lula took a little sip.

"Ain't too bad. Mite sweet, though. How you heard about 'em?"

"*Sex and the City*, the TV show? The girls on it are always meetin' up in a outdoor place like this, rushin' in breathless, then suckin' down a Cosmo as they commence complainin'."

"Complainin' about what?"

"Men, 'course. What else?"

"I never seen it."

"I missed it myself, first time around. Now I just catch the late at night reruns. Don't matter, you still got me to listen to."

"Thank goodness."

A waitress came to their table and asked, "You ladies ready for another?"

"Not quite yet," Beany answered. "You, Lula?"

Lula shook her head no.

"But I got a question," said Beany.

"Shoot," the waitress said.

"Why's this place called the Lion's Mouth?"

"Hebrews, 11:33. 'Who through faith subdued kingdoms, wrought righteousness, obtained promises, stopped the mouths of lions.' We're mostly God-fearin' folks around here, but you gotta have a place to let your hair down and this is as close as you get in Bay St. Clement."

The waitress walked away.

"Whew," said Beany, "she sure answered my question, didn't she?"

Lula nodded. "I only been here twice," she said.

Beany leaned forward and took Lula's left hand between both of her own.

"Lula, you know what we gotta do?"

"What?"

"Take a trip together."

"Where? When?"

"Now, tomorrow, or the next day. Don't matter much where. Let's just go to be goin'."

"Oh, Beany, quit. You mean take a sea cruise?"

"Hell, no. Them're for old folks. Anyway, I'd feel like a prisoner on a boat. We can drive."

"I don't know about you, Beany, but I gotta admit I'm feelin' shakey goin' on the interstate."

"Fine, we'll take back roads, go slow."

Beany still colored her hair. In the fading sunlight, Lula noticed, it had a greenish glow.

"Don't think I'm up to travelin', Beany. I'm happy these days just stickin' close to home."

"Lula, we're goin'! I won't let you set in a rockin' chair waitin' on the death ship."

"I'll think on it."

"We just gotta decide which way we're headed: up, down, or out west."

"Beany, I believe this Cosmo is makin' me dizzy. It and the heat."

"Okay, sweetie pie, we'll head back to Dal's, but by tomorrow mornin' we'll have a plan. We need an adventure, baby, bring out our inner girl."

"Beany, you're crazy."

Lula's oldest and best friend left in the world cackled and

said, "Board certified by the backwardest state in the entire confederacy."

"I don't know about that, Beany. Louisiana got itself some pretty stiff competition down here in the backwards department."

9

I guess its time I went back to NO. Pace tells me its a sorry sight since Katrina but this might be my last chance to see the city where I spent most of my life. I suppose I been reluctant to go since Sailor was killed I got so many memories there and hes in almost all. Beanys got my best interest in mind I know and this way Ill get to see my son. By the time Beany and I got back to the house from the Lions Mouth cafe she had pretty much made up my mind for me so I called Pace on his cell phone which as far as I know is the only number hes got. He didnt answer but I left him a message saying Im coming with Beany see you in a few days. I got his address in Metairie and if he aint got room for us to stay there Im sure we can find some hotel dont charge a arm or a leg. Beany herself aint been in NO for years she says and we can go on up to Plain Dealing after so I can see Hedy Lamarr and meet Delivery Music and their son Melton. Beany thinks Melton who dont have nothing better to do would drive me back to Bay St. Clement and then he can take a train back to Plain Dealing. It all sounds fine but I have to confess Im afraid being in NO again without Sail is gonna be tough. I could hardly stand it after he died thank goodness I had Dal to go to. After Mama passed I recalled what she had written to me from beside the deathbed of her old beau Marcello Santos. Marcello may have been a gangster Mama said but it werent all his fault hed done what he done because as it says in Kings he walked in all the way that his father walked in and served the idols that his father served and worshiped them. Santos may have done that which was evil in the sight of the Lord but he was set out on a path not of his choosing and at his very end he asked Mama to forgive him his ways cause he knew God would not. And Mama said she asked Marcello is thine heart right as my heart is with thy heart and he answered her it is so she said give me thine hand and he did and he was taken up into the chariot. Going to NO now might just be best help me conquer some shadows.

10

First thing this morning Beany and I drove over to Oscaritos Service to have my Mercury Nightcat checked out for the trip. That Oscarito is the nicest boy come up from Mexico about six years back with his brother Jose Pinto whos working now as a plasterer Oscarito tells me in Chicago. Oscarito hired on with old Dip Robinson at Dips Gulf Gas and now hes running the show. Dip is a good man but I aint unhappy he retired as this Oscarito is a ace mechanic. Oscarito says where he come from they couldnt afford to buy new parts so he learned how to make his own from leftovers. Even with all the computer stuff you gotta know now to make a car go he can work miracles with a wrench and a screwdriver. I believe if hed been assisting Doctor Frankenstein the monster would have come out right and never killed that little girl picking flowers. Beany and I left the Mercury with Oscarito walked over to the graveyard and talked about our route. Beany has it figured pretty well already we head for Myrtle Beach then Charleston to Beaufort down to Savannah and cross Georgia through Valdosta to Dothan Alabama and on into Mobile from there through Pascagoula Biloxi Gulfport Pass Christian whats left of it and then NO. Im steadying myself for a fright since Hurricane Katrina kicked ass along the gulf coast too. Beany says shes heard how the planet is getting too hot for humans and anyway pretty soon once all the ice melts up north they already got polar bears eating each other everyone living next to water will be under it. None of this news is easy to swallow maybe itll come down to what Isaiah said about hail sweeping away the refuge of lies and waters overflowing the hiding place because there wont be no place to hide people are either all in this boat together or there aint going to be no boat to be in.

II

"Lula, you about ready?"

"Comin'. I ain't so mobile as I used to be. Might be time for some replacement parts, I could afford 'em."

Lula came down the stairs slowly, keeping one hand on the bannister, carrying a small, brown, weatherbeaten valise in the other.

"That all you bringin', baby?" Beany asked.

Lula reached the bottom of the steps and put the valise down on the floor.

"This is Sailor's old getaway bag," she said. "I thought this's the proper occasion to use it. Holds all I'll need. I believe he'd be happy to know he's goin' back out on the road."

"What you mean 'he'?"

"Feel like Sailor's comin' with me, Beany, you know? Sail never went nowhere far from home he didn't take this valise."

"Elmo always insisted on takin' with him all he could. 'Never can tell when we'll be back, if ever,' he used to say. Man always was lookin' to move on, and that was a sign."

Lula held her tongue. She never had cared for Elmo, even when Beany'd been convinced he was the bee's knees, but she saw no earthly reason to add to her good friend's storehouse of ill thoughts concerning the man. After all, Lula thought, they'd soon be visiting with Elmo Pleasant's blood daughter, Hedy Lamarr, and who knew what memories she had of him. Most certainly Beany had long ago poisoned that well.

"Beany, before we get goin' there's one thing I gotta say."

"What's that, baby?"

"Back in the day Sailor and I were startin' out on a trip, it was his fiftieth birthday, drivin' across Lake Pontchartrain, time we encountered that strange girl, Consuelo Whynot."

"Teenager was mixed up with a lesbian Chickasaw in Miss'ippi, I recall. Killed a fella."

Lula nodded. "Wesley Nisbet, but it was Venus Tishomingo shot him, not Consuelo. Then Nisbet's car run Venus over."

"Sweet Jesus, like in that movie *Christine*. What about it?"

"Just that when we were on the bridge beginnin' that trip there was a bad sign Sail and I ignored. A big dead pelican fell from the sky and crashed on the roof of our Sedan de Ville. We'd understood it was a omen we would've turned around and gone back to N.O. Never woulda been involved with them crazy folks. Promise me, Beany, we get some kinda sign we stop right there, scoot back to Bay St. Clement."

"Okay, Lula, a dead pelican crashes on us, we'll turn back."

"Not just a pelican. I mean any weird incident could be a warnin'."

Beany stared into Lula's still bright gray eyes and held up her own right hand with the index and second fingers pressed together and the other two held down by her thumb.

"What's that?" asked Lula.

"Indian sign, means I promise. We good to go now?"

"Uh huh. Just I believe we're way too old for that sorta foolishness, Beany, don't you?"

12

We made pretty good progress today for two old women. We got kind of a late start but arrived in Myrtle Beach just after sunset. As we drove I couldnt help but think about Sailor and how when we were kids going to Myrtle Beach was about the end in the holiday department. Beany insisted on driving most of the way she goes faster than me of course. I called Pace again from a gas station by Calabash but got his message voice and left him one so at least he knows or will know when he listens to it that we really are on the road and headed his way. Beany is half decided to get herself a cell phone finally I guess its a good idea if your stuck on a highway at night with a flat tire or something but I keep resisting getting one as just one more modern piece of business to deal with. I hope I dont regret not having one I know it could be a lifesaver someday. So here we are in Myrtle Beach thank the Lord in off season so it was no trouble finding a place to stay. The Sunrise in Egypt Motel used to be was run by Betty Jane and Delmer Holden he was a distant cousin of the actor William Holden kept a poster of *The Wild Bunch* movie on the lobby wall. Thats gone now theres new owners but the rooms are clean. Sailor told me once he and a buddy Dodge Johnson whose daddy named him after his favorite car got stuck here for two days in a rainstorm and Dodge Johnson read the New Testament through about ten times out loud because he couldnt read silent and drove Sail almost crazy. Dodge claimed Revelations foretold the New Heaven and the New Earth was on another planet and that to get right with the Lord it was necessary to follow the Pure River and leave behind the dogs sorcerers whoremongers murderers idolators and liars who would all be condemned to dwell in New York City where Satan had reappeared following his thousand years of banishment from Gods Kingdom. Sailor never could stand to listen to anyone preach the New Testament after that but neither did he ever go to New York City.

13

"*Beany,* I'm afraid to go to N.O."

Beany was at the wheel and Lula was in the front passenger seat of the Nightcat at ten in the morning of a gray day as they motored slowly south on state highway 17 near Murrells Inlet.

"What're you sayin', baby?" asked Beany. "Afraid of what?"

"What we're gonna see. How wrecked the city is from the hurricane. I lived there forty years and I don't know if I could bear to see the place so torn up."

"You seen it on TV."

"Seein' somethin' on TV ain't the same as in person, Beany, you know that. I'm worried it'll break my heart."

Beany honked the horn at a black Cadillac Escalade in front of them that was moving too slowly and weaving out of its lane and back.

"Take it easy, there'll be a passin' lane in a minute."

"Natural disasters is part of life, Lula, it's why they're called natural. Hell, I'm a natural disaster myself, bein' in and out of mental institutions, mostly destroyin' my children's lives. It ain't difficult to see how the planet woulda been better off without the Good Lord planted me on it."

Tears rolled down Beany's cheeks. She wiped them away as she drove.

"Oh, Beany, darlin', that ain't true. You're one of God's rarest creatures and my dearest friend. Just you had a wild hair, is all, and couldn't always keep it in place."

"Yeah, like the most uncontrollable cowlick in the history of Crowley, Louisiana."

The road widened and Beany stabbed the accelerator pedal and zoomed the Mercury around the lumbering SUV.

"I was right, Lula. Look!"

As they sped by, Lula glimpsed the driver of the Escalade, a big-haired thirty-something holding a cell phone to her left ear.

"Is she smokin', too?" Beany asked.

"Can't tell. Oh, wait. Yep, she surely is. Got a long, thin ciggie between two fingers of her steerin' hand."

"You never smoke no more, Lula?"

"Ever' once in a while I puff on a Viceroy. 'Bout twice a month, maybe."

"Strange," said Beany, "smokin's about the only bad habit I didn't have, you know?"

"What you mean, 'didn't'? You still got time to develop one or two more mean deals before Armageddon."

Beany laughed. Her tears were gone.

"Wish Hedy Lamarr loved me the way you do, Lula, but I guess I get what I deserve. Deliver me from the hand of strange children, it says in Psalms."

"Like that teenager in Little Rock was on the news," Lula said, "decapitated his mother, a dog, and a parakeet."

Beany clucked her tongue. "You're right, Lula, things always could be worse."

14

When Lula took over the wheel at McClellanville, she asked Beany if she could borrow her sunglasses. Beany handed them over.

"Thanks, they're darker than mine," said Lula. "Glare here's bad."

"Amazin' you don't wear glasses 'cept to read," Beany said. "I can't get from the kitchen to the bathroom without mine."

"I got my mama's eyes, I guess. Marietta never wore any type of eyeglasses. I recall her readin' Eugene Sue's *Mysteries of Paris* to Marcello Santos when he was on his deathbed, didn't have on no spectacles."

"You're blessed. I started wearin' 'em when I couldn't read the writin' on the squares on the Monopoly board at Oriental."

"Did I ever tell you about Sailor's recurrin' dream involvin' a kind of board game?"

"No, Lula, what was it?"

"Well, it wasn't really on a board, it was on sand, on the ground. Sailor said the first time he had it he dreamed he was sittin' on the desert floor with a group of Indians, Hopis, perhaps, in the southwest somewhere, Arizona or New Mexico, and there was lines marked out in front of 'em, carved in the sand, creases like, and Sail and these Indians were movin' beads or stones, white rocks, from one place to another. He said they were sittin' on a mesa, all the colors were very bright, tan and beige and blue from the sky.

"After that, the second time he had the dream and the times after, the game was spread out over a much larger distance. There were more lines or creases drawn in the sand, shapes of figures like animals, and the beads or balls now, not stones or rocks, had to travel much further. Sailor told me he and the other players were sittin' with their legs folded underneath 'em on the ground and one of the rules was nobody could stand up to move any of the balls."

"Did he say how they moved?"

"Yes, this is the good part. They transported their pieces by mental telepathy, by the power of their mind. Ain't that somethin'?"

"Never heard nothin' like it. Did Sailor say if he won or not?"

"No, I don't believe winnin' was the object of the game.

Every time Sailor had this dream he told me it got more complicated and he couldn't really explain how the game was supposed to go, just the players bein' able to move the pieces with their thoughts was the important thing."

Beany shook her head. "Whew, I never knew Sailor had such a deep mind."

"He used to could surprise me, Beany. There was more to him than most people suspected. Sailor was a special boy."

"I'm glad you told me this, Lula. Puts Sailor in a whole different light."

"Beany, if I remember right, there used to be a good Dairy Queen in Wando we can stop at."

"Okay, baby, I could do with a strawberry double dip."

Sprinkles hit the windshield and Lula turned on the wipers.

"Oh, one more thing about Sailor's dream?"

"Tell, me."

"After he passed, I found a bunch of drawin's in his desk, markin's like the ones he described had been made in the sand in the Indian game."

"I guess he was tryin' to figure it out."

"Uh huh. That dream was a A-Number One mystery."

Beany nodded and said, "Sure as shootin', just like ever'thin' else."

15

After stopping for an ice cream in Wando and gassing up the Merc, Beany took the wheel for the busy stretch into Charleston.

"One night last week I couldn't sleep," said Lula, "so I turned on the TV and there was one of Sailor's favorite old black and white movies, *Virginia City*, with Errol Flynn and Humphrey Bogart as a Mexican bandit."

"Don't believe I ever seen it," Beany said. "Think I'd remember Bogey as a Mexican."

"He weren't real convincin'. Had a drawed on pencil-thin mustache and a bad accent, was weaselly-lookin'. That Errol Flynn, though, was just about scrumptious as a man could get. Makes all these skinny actors today look sick."

"I'm with you there, Lula. What's the picture about?"

"A Civil War western, where Randolph Scott—who was plenty cute, too, though Sail always said he was a three dollar bill—is with our side and he's sent to Virginia City, Nevada, to get gold to finance the Confederacy. Flynn's a Yankee undercover agent out to stop him. He does, but he likes Scott so doesn't let the Union have the gold, which he buries under a rockslide. Bogart's got a gang of filthy desperadoes ridin' around robbin' everybody. Best part of the movie, though, is when Flynn's double does a header on horseback over a cliff."

"Who's the girl? That simpy, Goody Two-Shoes person always about to faint ever' time Errol noticed her?"

"You mean Olivia de Havilland. No, she was much prettier than this one. This is a dancehall gal workin' for the rebels who's only a half-attractive blonde with doll-baby ringlets, sort of a third-rate American Marlene Dietrich. Had an annoyin' voice, too. I'll bet even Flynn didn't put it to her."

A light rain persisted but Beany kept her window down. "I like feelin' the soft drops while I drive," she said. "It's like they're pokin' me to keep payin' attention to the road."

Lula kept her window cracked slightly just to catch a tiny breeze.

"But Lula? My best guess is ol' Errol had all his leadin' ladies like chickens-in-the-basket. Them actors and actresses are always at it. I read in some magazine years ago a interview with John Derek—one was married to Bo

Derek?—where he said he made fifty movies and durin' each one he went to bed with the actress played opposite him. He said it was expected by the director—unless the director was gunnin' her, too—and, most of all, by the actress her own self, made her more confident. 'Course it helped Derek that he was about the prettiest boy when he was young, even more than that French actor looks so queeny now. Read how he goes to Tahiti every couple years for a face lift."

"Yeah, I guess so," said Lula. "But I like to think even in Hollywood there's true romance once in a while."

"You don't think you woulda cheated on Sailor with Errol Flynn?"

"Uh uh, Beany, not a chance. Can't say I wouldn't have appreciated the offer, but I knew Sail was my man since I was sixteen years old. Even when he was sent up for pullin' that feed store holdup in Texas with that devil Bobby Peru, I stayed true. Also when we was separated after. I believed in my heart it was in the stars that we was meant to be together forever."

Beany sighed and said, "Lula, that's so precious. I believe you, I always have. But even if I'd been as lucky with a man as you were with Sailor Ripley, I wouldn'ta passed on Errol Flynn."

16

I been thinking lately about my daddy how my life might have been different had he not died so early in it. No doubt he would not have approved of my marrying Sailor no more than Mama did so Im certain we would have had a powerful disagreement in that department. I like to think on him sitting in his favorite chair the one with the ripped up armrests torn apart by my cat Blue Eyed Jane named after Daddys specialmost Jimmie Rodgers song. He loved to listen to those old records of Jimmies his granddaddy give him he had em all on 78. Nobody did Jimmie right Daddy said so he made this music that would last as long as anyones and then died from TB. Why Should I Be Lonely had the words I preferred the best of all. Why should I be so lonely why should I be sad though another is taking from me the best pal Ive ever had shes taking the sunshine with her leaving the clouds for me but why should I be so lonesome when theres nobody lonesome for me. This describes my feeling for Sailor having fallen into the embrace of Madame Death who Sail said would be my only rival. How could I know when I was a child and listened to those songs with my daddy that Jimmie had already saw Madame standing in the shadows.

17

Beany and I spent the night at the Henry Nimrod B &
B in Charleston and when I woke up this morning Beany
had left me a note saying shed already gone down to breakfast. Imagine my surprise when I found her sitting at a table
with a beautiful boy who looked about sixteen but as it
turns out is twenty three. His name of all things is Epistro-
phy Trane Taylor but goes by his initials ET. He was staying
at the Nimrod for a couple of days while exploring
Charleston hes from Lake Charles Louisiana. Told us his
mama and daddy are jazz people so named him after their
favorite tune by Monk and middle name after Coltrane. He
was just a little kid when the movie ET come out so it was
a natural to be called that and it stuck. ET has long wavy
light brown hair and green eyes you can imagine looking in
em and seeing a jungle lagoon with crocodiles gliding along.
You really could get a little lost staring in there I cant

explain it better. Anyway Beany seen him and the breakfast room was filled so she asked ET if she could sit at the table with him and he jumped right up and pulled out a chair for her. Turns out ET graduated college last June now its October and has been traveling around by bus and thumb for almost four months trying to figure out what he wants to do with his life. Hes been to the midwest and up and down the east coast sometimes doing small jobs the usual. His degree from of all places Daniel Schmutz University in Switzerland is in computer science so ET could work anywhere with his skills but he says he cant stand the idea of sitting at a desk in front of a computer screen all day I dont blame him a bit. We asked how it was he went to school over there in Switzerland especially being from Lake Charles he said his grandparents live there its where his mama grew up in those mountains. She met his daddy on a holiday trip to NO and they run off together got married she was eighteen and they been living in his daddys home town of Lake Charles ever since. ETs daddy is a car mechanic with his own garage and a trumpet player on the side. His mama runs the business and paints pictures of flowers mostly also she plays the cello. Besides English ET speaks German his mama taught him growing up she didnt speak English hardly at all when she run into ETs daddy to be. His name is Alastair Taylor his family being originally from Scotland but ET says everybody calls his daddy Duke because of Duke Ellington its the name of the garage Dukes. ET told us hes running real low on money and is hitching his way to Lake Charles so Beany said he could ride with us to NO without asking me not that I would have said no. He accepted and went to get his things from his room just a pack and a guitar. After ET was gone Beany whispered to me not to panic but this boy made her wet at least feel she could be wet then laughed crazy out loud so everybody stared. I been writing this waiting in the car for her and here she is with ET carrying our bags. I got a feeling something out of my control is going on but is it a sign?

18

"*I been* readin' this book I picked up in Atlanta, *Why God Don't Need to Carry a Gun.* Says people ought just listen to their inner voice so there can be peace in the world."

"What's this inner voice sayin'?" Beany asked ET. She was driving. Lula was in the front passenger seat and ET was in the back, strumming on his Gibson Hummingbird.

"It's the Lord's message comin' through His angels, is what it is. A person's body is sort of a celestial radio station. You got to get tuned in to His frequency."

"You mean the angels are broadcastin' for Him from inside us?" asked Beany.

"God's disc jockeys," said ET, and strummed a G major chord. "They're pluckin' on your heartstrings like they do on their harps, singin' 'Babylon is fallen, is fallen, the Lord's son is callin', is callin'. He who worships the beast and his image shall carry his mark, and dwell ever after without rest in the dark.'"

"You really believe this, ET?" Lula asked. "What it says in this book?"

"I guess so."

"There ain't no guessin' when it comes to religion," said Lula.

ET sang, accompanying himself on his guitar: "Oh God don't need to carry a gun/ And you know He ain't the only one/ No, you and I can be in His number, too/ Lambs and lions and beasts of burden/ Us creatures commanded by His word and/ Then we'll all be raptured with His son."

"Never heard that hymn before," said Beany.

"I know," said ET, "I wrote it myself. Glad as gravy you gals give me a ride. I knew as soon as I seen you both together that it was a sign."

Lula rolled down her window all the way and let the breeze hit her full in the face.

19

Somewhere around the turnoff for Edisto Island, Lula drifted off to sleep and dreamed that she was her much younger self alone on a beach at sunset. Suddenly, a big red wave rose up and crashed on the ground in front of her and as the water receded revealed human body parts lying on the sand. Arms, legs, what looked like a neck, even a few heads littered the beach. She was jolted out of this daytime nightmare by a bump.

"Sorry," said Beany, "couldn't dodge some possum remains."

Lula recognized the tune playing on the radio, "Little Rain" by Jimmy Reed. Sailor had always said that this was the slowest blues song ever recorded. "Old Jimmy done gone catatonic on this one," Lula recalled Sailor saying, as the singer slurred the line, "Little rain keep a-fallin' on this here love of mine."

She looked over her left shoulder and saw that ET was

sitting with his legs folded, his fingers forming a teepee, and his eyes closed.

"He's meditatin'," Beany told her. "Says he does it twice a day. Told me while you were snoozin' that if ever'body in the world meditated at precisely the same time every day, there wouldn't be no more war."

"He might be right."

Lula reached into the back seat and picked up ET's copy of *Why God Don't Need to Carry a Gun.* ET did not notice since he was still in a trance.

"Listen here what it says, Beany: 'When the king of Israel was in Samaria, there was a famine and a woman said unto him, "Give thy son, that we may eat him today, and we will eat my son tomorrow." So the king gave up his son and they boiled and ate him. When on the next day the king asked the woman for her son, she hid him. The king of Israel took no vengeance upon this woman, but instead mourned the loss of his son for all to see. Do you think the king of Israel's unselfish act was an inspiration to his people, or do you think he was just stupid to have allowed the woman to trick him? Do you think the woman should have been punished for her deception? Do you believe cruelty born out of desperation is justified? If you were God, would you have acted to rectify the situation?'"

"If I was God, I wouldn'ta done nothin'," said ET, who had emerged from his trance.

"You wouldn'ta restored the king of Israel's son to life?" asked Lula.

"Nope. This way it becomes an act that nobody would forget, and the story told and re-told as it has been on down the line as a lesson of supreme generosity."

"Generosity my ass," said Beany. "Myself, I woulda had that bitch boiled and eaten."

They rode for a few minutes in silence, each absorbed by their thoughts, then Lula said, "My deceased husband, Sailor Ripley, liked to quote the dyin' words of some Spanish general: 'I do not have to forgive my enemies. I have had them all shot.'"

"That'll work," Beany said.

"Mm-mm," said ET, "maybe age got somethin' to do with how a person thinks about things."

20

I clearly can remember how I felt surrounded by Sailors big strong arms. This memory will never leave me. The three times Sail and I got back together namely after he was sprung from Pee Dee after serving his time for manslaughtering Bob Ray Lemon then when he was released after being in Huntsville following the feed store robbery in Texas and finally after we once and for always was reunited during the time Pace was kidnapped in NO on each occasion without talking when he crushed me to his chest I melted into him and no words could ever describe this peaceful feeling. Home for me was in that mans arms and I aint been home since Sailor Ripley left this planet. Now with Beany and the boy ET we are stopped at a service station in Beaufort ET is gassing up the car and Beany is in the restroom. Im looking forward to seeing Pace as I am feeling a little bit low at the moment probably because I am so used to being alone so even though I love Beany dearly and she always means well it tires me out to be so long in her company or I guess anybodys. ET aint no trouble hes just lost as are so many these days. This was true of Sailor and Pace too for some time until they both got it figured out it took a while they had to learn there aint no rules in the game of life. ET told me hes always felt like a stranger loosed upon the world unwanted sent to Switzerland and all and I said Pace and me felt that way after Sailor was taken from us so early and sudden. I quoted scripture cursed be he that perverteth the judgment of the stranger the fatherless and the widow which covers us three dont it you got to follow your heart and dont despair no matter how creepy things get. Here comes Beany.

21

"*C'mon,* Lula, have some fun!"

"I am havin' fun, Beany. You go on and dance, I just enjoy watchin'."

Lula, Beany, and ET were in Hollywood Del's, a night-club on the outskirts of Savannah. Beany had been dancing with ET to Felix Mendelssohn and His Sepia Cats, a band that specialized in '60s soul music. Just now they had launched into "Shotgun," the old Junior Walker & the All-Stars tune. ET went to the bar to get himself another beer and Beany plopped down in a chair next to Lula's.

"I like they're playin' oldies, Lula, honey, 'cause I can't get into this hip rap, or rap hop, or whatever they call it. Whew! It's a wonder I can even move out there on the dance floor. You catch me tryin' to do the skate?"

Lula laughed. "You're amusin' and amazin', Beany, you

truly are. Somebody'd knock into me, I'd go flyin' and end up in the hospital with a busted hip."

"Lula, I know I'm an old lady, but d'you think it'd offend ET if I asked him to go to bed with me just once?"

It took Lula a few seconds to realize that Beany was deadly serious, then she said, "Hard to say. I know the very thought kinda offends me."

"Why? I ain't expectin' a miracle, only it'd be sorta sweet to have some affection of the intimate type."

"Beany, it might could take a miracle for that boy to get an erection in your presence, and even if he did you'd break apart soon as he squeezed you."

Beany took a swig from her bottle of Pabst Blue Ribbon and shook her head. "It's embarrassin' to be horny at eighty," she said.

"Ladies, meet Jamilla."

Lula and Beany looked up to see ET with a dark-skinned young woman.

"She's from—Where is it you're from again?"

"Nazareth," said Jamilla. "That's in Israel. I'm an Arab Israeli."

"'And Joseph came and dwelt in a city called Nazareth: that it might be fulfilled which was spoken by the prophets. He shall be called a Nazarene.' That's from Matthew, 'course. Nice to meet you, Jamilla. I'm Lula and my friend here is Beany."

Beany gave Jamilla a tiny wave. "World's oldest teenager."

"We're gonna go dance," said ET, taking the girl by the hand.

"Well, I guess that answers my question," Beany said. "Look at her, she sure is shapely. Shoot, I hate bein' ancient."

"Beany, you gotta try to get comfortable with it or you'll be miserable all the rest of your days."

"What you think of all these female teachers seducin' their boy students lately? Some are even havin' babies by 'em."

As Felix Mendelssohn and His Sepia Cats segued from "Shotgun" into "Green Onions," Lula watched Jamilla and ET take it down a notch and slither easily into scratch 'n' sniff mode.

"I don't think the world is so wild at heart any more, Beany, just weird on top. Probably each generation on its way out thinks what's come after them is missin' a bulb and dimmer for it. Then again, maybe it's just us old folks can't see so good and it hurts us to admit it."

"Lula, stop."

"Stop what?"

"Sayin' 'us old folks.' I plain can't stand it, even I know this is true."

Lula placed one of her hands over one of Beany's on the table. Tears rolled down Beany's cheeks.

"When the angels call and ask me to recall the thrill of them all, then I shall tell them I remember you."

Beany smiled and used her free hand to wipe away the tears.

"What part of the Bible's that from?" she asked.

"Ain't. It's words from an old song Mama and Dal liked."

"Thanks, baby, but it's Sailor you'll tell the angels about, not me."

Beany picked up Lula's hand and kissed it, then looked for ET and Jamilla on the dance floor. They weren't there.

22

At nine o'clock the next morning, Lula and Beany were dressed and ready to get back on the road. They had made coffee on the Mister Coffee machine in their room at The 4 Queens Motel located on the business loop of highway 95, availed themselves of four complimentary powdered dough-nuts which Beany had brought back from the lobby, and dialed ET's room twice but had no answer.

"He's probably off somewheres with his Jewess. What you think, Lula?"

"She's an Arab, Beany, not a Jew. Think about what?" Lula was still sipping her second cup of watery Folger's.

"How long should we wait?"

"Hate to say it, but if ET ain't come around by the time we set to roll, he'll have to catch his self another ride."

"What I think, also."

Fifteen minutes later, as the two women were putting

their bags into the Merc, the telephone rang in their room. The door was open. Lula went back in.

"Mornin', ET. Yeah, we're on the verge. Guess we could, but no longer. Glad you understand. See you shortly, then."

Beany and Lula were leaning up against the side of the car watching storm clouds form to the east when a metallic green Dodge Dart rumbled into the motel parking lot and stopped next to the Nightcat. Jamilla, wearing blue jean cutoffs clean to the bikini line and a red halter top, got out from the driver's side while ET exited the passenger side.

"Sorry I'm a little late, ladies," he said, "but Jammy and I didn't get to her crib until past four."

Beany took one look at ET and shouted, "Damn, boy! What in creation happened to you?"

With his right hand, ET gingerly fingered the blackened area around his right eye.

"Had a brief scuffle with a former suitor of Jammy's. He followed us to her place from Hollywood Del's and sucker punched me."

Jamilla had on dark glasses with fake rhinestones decorating the frames.

"He hit you, too?" Beany asked.

Jamilla just shook her head no and kept her back to the Dart.

"I'll get my pack and guitar and we can be goin'," said ET, and headed toward his motel room.

"Hope you made it worth his while," Beany said to Jamilla, who remained mute, her hands stuck in the back pockets of her shorts.

"Beany, quit," said Lula.

"You sure got pretty legs, though," Beany said.

"How do you like livin' in Savannah, Jamilla?" Lula asked. "Compared to Israel, I mean."

"They got fightin' here, too," said Beany.

Jamilla did not respond. ET came back, carrying his things, which he set down on the ground next to Lula's car. He went over to Jamilla.

"It's all good, huh, baby?" he said to her. "My eye'll be fine. I'll holler at you from Lake Charles."

ET leaned in to kiss her and Jamilla brought out a push-button stiletto from her left back pocket and shoved the blade hard into ET's abdomen. She kept her hand on it and twisted the knife before he fell, then lost her grip.

Lula and Beany could not believe this had happened. Neither of them made a sound. They stood frozen as Jamilla opened the driver's side door of her car, climbed in, started it up, threw the shiny green machine into reverse and backed away. The two women watched the Dodge Dart fishtail out of the lot and roar onto business 95, then they dropped down and kneeled on either side of ET's prostrate body. His eyes were open and his lips were still puckered up, expecting to be kissed. Lula pushed the tips of the index and middle fingers of her right hand against the carotid artery of ET's neck, held them there for a few seconds, then looked up into Beany's eyes.

"This is worse than weird," said Lula.

23

I been sitting in our room number 8 at The 4 Queens Motel just thinking about everything thats happened and listening to the radio. When I was a girl I listened a lot to the radio it seems like back then it was something more people did just sit and listen and dream and maybe there wasnt no more good news then than there is now but it didnt seem like things was moving so fast that every time a person stepped out the door the world was a different place than when you went inside. Beany has been spending time with Mr and Mrs Taylor ETs parents since they come to get their sons body and take it back to Lake Charles. I guess they are going to have the corpse shipped by railroad they cant take it in their Sedan de Ville. If this had happened to Pace when he was so young as ET I dont know what I would have done probably felt like killing myself but I wouldnt because of Sailor. We gave the Savannah police our eyewitness testimony to the murder and two days later the highway patrol spotted Jamillas car in Fernandina Beach parked at a Steak and Shake and arrested her and a forty year old man named Hamid Khartoum who told the authorities he was Jamillas fiance. This must have been the same one hit ET that night we met her at Hollywood Dels nightclub but Im not certain. Jamilla confessed to the killing her fingerprints was of course on the knife so there aint going to be a trial only a sentence which will likely be for life. Her fiance will get time for being a accessory after the fact for helping her escape. Its all too terrible and reminds me too much of the bad business in Big Tuna all the years ago. The Taylors are good people and devastated. Beany told me Jamilla her last name is Salim said she stabbed poor ET because she says he defiled her body those are the words she used. Beany knows more details but I told her honestly I dont need to hear any. The girl is crazy out of her freaking mind and this Hamid Khartoum is some moron under her thumb. A cute tune I heard on the radio a moment ago is a new version of Put Your Head On My Shoulder the old Paul Anka song done by a group called Blue Mother Tupelo its just the sweetest and sexiest record I believe Sailor would have dug it to death. The girl doing the vocal can really sing too sort of warbly she reminds me a bit of Patsy on I Fall to Pieces mixed with the way Brenda did Heart in Hand both favorites of mine and Sailors. This music is personal as opposed to that stuff could be anybody or nobody just some machine. Sailor said the record companies sometimes produce music they think will be commercial with equipment then hire people to pretend its theirs and have them on a video like actors. I want to hear a real person whispering the song in my ear. Theres the phone. It was Beany saying the police are letting us continue on our way tomorrow they have our written statements its all they need. Thank goodness we wont have to testify in a courtroom. I called Pace yesterday he answered and I told him what happened and he said he never told me but when he was married to Rhoda Gombowicz and living in New York they were attacked one night in front of their building by two men with knives took Paces wallet and Rhodas purse then one of the men stabbed Pace in his left leg on the thigh so he wouldnt run after them. Rhoda took Pace to a hospital they stitched him up and he made Rhoda promise never to tell me and Sailor so we wouldnt worry about him being in New York as if there werent no crime in New Orleans. Matthew says from the days of John the Baptist until now the kingdom of heaven suffereth violence and the violent take it by force. This is a fact of life I been touched so many times by violence what to do but bear it and bless them who are less blessed than others. Pace said to come on hes got a nice little apartment above a courtyard on Orleans Street in the Quarter for Beany and me to stay at and dont pick up no more stray boys on the road. In the newspaper Rashid Salim Jamillas daddy said she only done what was right by their law and that he would have killed ET if she had not. I wonder if Mister Salim ever seen his daughter wearing next to nothing like on the day she stuck ET.

24

"*Ain't* seen you so quiet since that time I visited you in the bin and you was drugged dumb."

"Tell you, Lula, God's truth, it took all my energy and more just to try accomodatin' and consolin' Duke and Lady Taylor. Their guts is twisted, their hearts are broke and their brains been blasted by a A-bomb."

Lula and Beany were near Willacoochee, Georgia, halfway between Waycross and Tifton. It was a sunny day but colder than normal, not a cloud in the sky.

"That ET's mama's name, Lady?"

"It's really Ladina but Duke calls her Lady, so ever'body else in Lake Charles does, too. Suppose when she's back in Switzerland she's called Ladina."

"Sorry I wasn't more helpful to 'em, Beany, and to you, too, but I just could barely stand it myself. I been through plenty, as you know, but the shock of seein' that girl stick

ET right in front of our eyes done somethin' to me I can't rightly describe."

"Made you sick, is what it did. Sure did me. I kept up for ET's folks' sakes, is all. Horrible the way his beautiful green eyes was emptyin' out when he was on the ground, life leakin' like anti-freeze into the earth."

Lula's eyes were fixed steady on state highway 82. She felt Marietta's presence, as if her mama were sitting in the car next to her instead of Beany. Marietta wasn't such a difficult person as most people thought, Lula had decided. She just knew what she wanted and was tough-minded about it. Lula was not so tough, not like that, never had been. She wished that the murdering whore Jamilla Salim had not been wearing dark glasses when she stabbed ET. Lula thought that she would have liked to have seen her eyes at precisely the moment the blade entered ET's body. After Jamilla and Hamid had been taken into custody in Fernandina Beach, Lula had seen her on the TV news sitting in the back seat of a highway patrol car. Jamilla, still wearing dark glasses, had stuck out her tongue at the reporters and photographers and Lula remembered being stunned at how incredibly long it was, the longest tongue by far that she had ever seen.

25

The trip has pretty much been a blur since we left Savannah and now we just got to Dothan Alabama where Sailors daddy lived at one time and worked as a colporteur hawking bibles and other religious items door to door. This was before Sailor was born he told me even before his mama met his daddy. Sailor had some family in this state but he didnt keep in touch and we never visited or wrote. I always had a strong feeling for family but not Sail except for me and Pace of course and as long as he and Mama kept a decent distance from one another they was all right. Just now the song Stars Fell on Alabama come into my head the way Billie Holiday sung it with that crackly wrinkle in her voice My heart beat like a hammer my arms wound around you tight and stars fell on Alabama last night. Sailor used to say she was a sly singer knew right when to put her toe in the water. Beanys been unearthly silent until this evening when she got into it on the telephone with Hedy Lamarr seems Hedy found out her husband Delivery Music been giving free produce from his market to a 18 year old name of Jacey Spikes whos a member of their church Rock Hard Baptist shes the singer for a Christian band called Rock Hard. Delivery says there aint no hanky panky in it hes just helping out a poor girl and her family. Hedy told Beany this Jacey Spikes was responsible for their previous minister having to leave after his wife found nude pictures of Jacey on his computer she was fourteen then now shes five foot eight with platinum blonde hair and titties out to there. Beany asked Hedy if she had any proof of Delivery carrying on behind her back and Hedy said no but that this girl was such an attraction male attendance at their church gone up by more than half since Rock Hard been performing on Sundays. Some of the wives complained to the minister Reverend Swindle who Hedys convinced is a secret morphine addict has a strange close friendship with a local Doctor Caldwell but he told them the collection baskets reflect overwhelming approval of most worshippers end of discussion. Dont ride herd too close on your man Beany said to Hedy or your liable to get a horn in your leg better to let Delivery have his fantasy at his age he aint very likely to start something he most probably cant finish anyway. Out the window of our room at the Hotel Lurleen I can see

74

smokestacks shooting shit high into the dark sky theres gold silver and other colors sparkling in the blackness its beautiful but probably are particles cause cancers lung disease and allergies. Lord it seems everywhere you look theres something to worry about I know what Sailor would say so dont look.

26

Beany had the wheel and following her conversation with Hedy Lamarr had regained some of her energy. She was doing her best to dismiss from her thoughts the unfortunate episode in Savannah. She and Lula were cruising in the Merc past cottonfields on state route 84 in a steady drizzle.

"Once I saw Wilson Pickett, who for my money was the funkiest, down and flat out dangerous-seemin' soul singer of 'em all," said Beany, "on a TV show. He was from Alabama and had gone as a young man up to live in Detroit, where he stayed. The interviewer asked him had he ever been back to Alabama and Pickett got wicked on the spot, said he'd been booked to perform in Tuscaloosa, I believe, and was on the way there from the airport in Birmingham, but when the car started passin' cottonfields he freaked out, told the driver to turn around and take him back to the airport. His memories of havin' to pick cotton as a child hit him harder than he could have imagined, he couldn't take it. 'Ninety-nine and a half just won't do!' Pickett shouted, like in his song. 'Ninety-nine and a half won't cut it! Gotta be I'm one hundred per cent or I'm out the game!'"

"Poor man," said Lula. "I can understand not wantin' to go back somewhere somethin' awful happened to you. For instance, I ain't in all this time been back to Texas, nor will I ever go."

Rain began falling harder.

"Mind if I cut on the heater?" Beany asked.

"Please do. I just felt a little shiver myself."

"That's what Wilson Pickett was doin' on that TV show, shiverin', soon as he heard the word Alabama. It'll prob'ly happen to us now, Lula, whenever someone says Savannah."

Lula could not help but think how beautiful the cotton-fields looked in the rain.

27

I just now switched off the TV in our room at the Chickasaw Motor-In. Beany done most of the driving today so shes been sleeping for a couple hours but Im more restless than usual. Watching and listening to the news dont help calm me it never does but I got to admit its hard not to think the world is in the worst shape probably since WW2 and no doubt worse since now with the kinds of weapons almost anyone can get their hands on it wouldnt take but a few minutes for the entire planet to explode and almost all its creatures to expire. Pace never has had no kids so I dont have any grandbabies to worry about Ive always been a little maybe sometimes more than a little sad about that but now Im thinking Im not because of how theyd have to be living in this messed up time in history. Sailor read to me once a story about how after a nuclear war the people who remain half of them live above the ground and the other half beneath in caves. The ones in the beneath who are ugly and beastly and never see the light of day control the ones above who are all beautiful cause of course they have sunlight and flowers and fresh air and eat fruit and vegetables. The beneath people are really raising the outdoors ones like cattle to eat. Whenever they need to have a feast the beneath creatures turn on a loud siren that hypnotizes the healthy outside ones who all march like zombies toward the place the loud noise is coming from its the entrance to the cave where the beast people are waiting and when enough of the healthy pretty people have gone down that day the siren stops and the cave door closes. Then the beautiful dumb ones come out of their trances and go back to their perfect seeming life like nothing is wrong and they dont miss the ones gone under to be devoured by the beneath people. In the end I think a volcano explodes and covers everything and the beneath folks are cooked below and the up top people are boiled alive by a flood of hot lava. So both groups are wiped out and thats the end of civilization. Now we got a situation where all these different countries think they got the right answer or religion including of course our own and I dont believe nobody does some are more greedy than others and more righteous but a person in a mountain hut in Asia got just as much right to their version of the way things ought to be as one in LA thinks more about her tan line than one who might be starving in a desert covered by flies in Africa. And here at home we got demented men shooting down children in schools and politicians in Washington DC supposed to be our leaders molesting boys and girls its just like Rome was in the long ago I believe. My question now is of those who will be left on this planet after the bombs and missiles go off which ones go beneath and who stays above. I know the presidents and dictators already have underground places with food and guns stashed away to go to so it aint really no big mystery who the beneath people would be. And when their food supply runs out they got the guns and going cannibal aint a stretch. I would choose to be above if I could but not if the beneath could control my mind. Its late and we want to drive from Mobile to NO tomorrow so Ill quit and try to sleep some. Maybe before everything goes forever ass over backwards as crazy old Coot Veal Sailors hunting buddy used to put it about a million years ago people everywhere will come to their senses and stop their feuding and bad behavior but I hate to say I doubt it. I think this version of civilization is already tipped over too far to get right and there aint no way in anyones heaven or hell to keep us poor fools from being ramroded down the chute. In Pauls second letter to the Thessalonians he wrote And to you who are troubled rest with us when the Lord Jesus shall be revealed from heaven with his mighty angels in flaming fire taking vengeance on them that know not God and who shall be punished with everlasting destruction. Well Im troubled but cant rightly rest believing how I do that there aint going to be no selection about who shall be destroyed.

28

Lula made sure that she and Beany got an early start the next day, which was Sunday, October eighth.

"Elmo, he was a big baseball fan," said Beany, "maybe you remember. Anyway, October the eighth is a date I can't forget 'cause it's the anniversary of the day in 1956 Don Larsen of the New York Yankees pitched the only perfect game in the history of the World Series. Elmo'd been a Yankee fan from since he was a boy and that was a big day for him. Used to he'd get in fights with kids all the time around Natchitoches, where he grew up, he told me, because of his likin' the Yankees. Most of the other kids rooted for the Saint Louis Cardinals because back then they were the only team from the South or closest to, bein' that Missouri was a border state. I never was much of a fan myself but those times I got socked away at Oriental, I used to listen to baseball games on the radio. They had it on and it soothed me some, kept me calm just to know somewhere out in the world things was just goin' on the way they was supposed to. Stan Musial would double down the right field line, the crowd would be makin' noise and there wasn't nothin' to argue about. It was just a double, and that was that."

"It was the drugs kept you calm," said Lula, "more'n the baseball."

"Combination, I guess."

Lula stayed on the old highway, keeping the Mercury in the slow lane on purpose in order to take a good look at what Katrina had done to the Mississippi Gulf Coast.

"Heard the wind was so powerful it moved the casino buildin's in Biloxi back off their foundations," said Beany.

They were cruising through Pascagoula but there wasn't much to see in the way of damage. There were plenty of trucks carrying building materials on the road, however.

"People here're pretty strong," Lula said. "I don't know how I'd do if a hurricane carried off ever'thin' I owned. Wonder could I find it in myself to tough it out or just move on, start new somewheres else."

"Hard to say."

"After Sailor was killed, I kinda felt like I didn't want or need anything. Mean I didn't much care about possessions, didn't want to look at old photos, stuff like that."

"You had Pace."

Lula nodded. "'Course, I did, and he was a big help to me, but it didn't take much for me to decide to leave New Orleans and go live with Dal. Pace took most of Sailor's stuff, sold the house and made sure all the finances was in order. Dal couldn'ta been kinder, also. I had it pretty easy, a place to go and all. Nothin' like the folks down here had to face after Katrina."

"After the big hurricane in the Florida Keys in 1935?" said Beany. "They had more'n a thousand men workin' on buildin' the highway through there and didn't get 'em out in time. Weeks and months later bodies were found hangin' from trees and in the mangroves around Islamorada. Tidal wave swamped the train sent down from Miami to evacuate everyone. Eight hundred people died."

"Storm musta been the size of Katrina," said Lula.

Now on both sides of the road from Ocean Springs to Waveland were piles of debris, and behind them what was left of the houses and buildings that had lined Highway 90.

"Wonder if the old Wildrose house in Pass Christian was destroyed," said Beany.

"You mean that giant black wooden one with the fancy wraparound porch and parapets and towers and outside staircases?"

"Yeah. The one where the little girl was kidnapped from like the Lindbergh baby."

"They found her, though, right?" said Lula. "The Wildrose girl."

"Uh huh, but practically suffocated to death in a steamer trunk on a wharf in N.O. Men who took her were arrested tryin' to get on a ship to Brazil, had the ransom money on 'em. Remember seein' a picture of the kidnappers in handcuffs next to one of nine-year-old Mabel Wildrose on the front page of the *Picayune*. Two bald guys with black mustaches wearin' bush jackets."

Suddenly the sky became smoky. Sunlight penetrated the haze in narrow shafts.

"Where's all this smoke comin' from? You see all right, Lula?"

"Must be a fire nearby. Burnin' debris, maybe."

"That girl Mabel Wildrose?" said Beany. "One who was kidnapped?"

"What about her?"

"She lived to be one hundred years old. Lived all the rest of her life in the house in Pass Christian."

"She's lucky she didn't have to live to see it smashed in the hurricane."

Beany nodded, then said, "I'm glad as blazes nobody ever took me and locked me up in a steamer trunk when I was a little girl. I'll bet Miss Wildrose never got it out of her mind for the next ninety years."

29

As they approached the Huey P. Long Bridge on their way into New Orleans, Lula began to cry.

"What is it, baby?" asked Beany.

"It's why I made you drive this last stretch," said Lula. "This is where Sailor met his demise, on the Old Spanish Trail."

"Oh, sweetness, of course it is. You go on and sob, then. You don't mind, though, I'll cut on OZ, get us some local sounds."

Sonny Rollins' strident tenor barked at them from the radio as Beany nosed the Nightcat onto the bridge.

"Wowee! I was expectin' Mac or Irma, not this bughouse bad boy!"

Beany switched the station and settled on the 1946 Xavier Cugat Orchestra playing "Perfidia."

"Listen to them strings, Lula. Sounds like rain slidin' down windows to the soul."

They drove without talking the rest of the way across the bridge.

As they left the river behind them, Beany asked, "What's that address Pace give you? I forgot it."

Lula struggled to regain her composure and said, "Orleans Street, number 926. Close by Burgundy, I believe."

When they got to the Quarter, Beany remarked, "Ever'thin' looks so normal. Never know there'd ever been a hurricane here."

"It's mostly everywhere else got pasted, 'specially the Lower Nine. Pace says it's a ghost town over to St. Bernard."

"Yeah, saw on CNN Fats Domino's house was submerged. The shotgun, anyway, not that motel-type structure behind."

"Heard he got rescued off the roof by a helicopter."

They were surprised to find a parking place on Orleans directly across the street from 926.

"What's the woman's name owns it?" Beany asked as they got out of the car.

Lula opened her purse and found the little piece of paper on which she'd written the information Pace had given her.

"Marnie Kowalski. Pace said she's a good lookin' little blonde, about forty. Lives in the front house and rents out two rear apartments overlook the courtyard."

"Girlfriend of his?"

"Maybe, but I don't think he's keepin' special company these days."

Lula pressed the buzzer marked Kowalski. She pressed it again thirty seconds later.

"One of you gals Pace Ripley's mama?"

Lula and Beany looked up and saw a woman's head sticking out of an upstairs window. Her hair was blonde and clipped short.

"She is," said Beany.

The head disappeared for a few seconds, then reappeared.

"Catch!" the woman said, and tossed down a key, which landed on the sidewalk.

Beany picked up the key and said to the woman, "You Marnie Kowalski?"

"Marnie as in Hitchcock and Kowalski out of Tennessee Williams. Let yourselves in. I'm buildin' a gumbo up here."

Just as Beany had turned the key in the front door lock and she and Lula were about to enter the house, someone spoke to them.

"Y'all live here?"

Beany and Lula looked around and saw a short, thin, dusty bituminous-colored girl of about twelve or thirteen wearing a red dress with white polkadots standing on the sidewalk.

"Who're you?" asked Lula.

"Eclair Feu, French for fire. Used to I lived on Mystery Street, close by Esplanade. I'm almost fourteen years old. My house was destroyed in the flood and my mama and baby sister, Byzantina, livin' now in Texas, I think."

"Don't you have any other family here?" Beany asked.

Eclair wore her hair in braids and they whipped around as she shook her head. "Naw, everyone gone or drown."

"Why didn't you go to Texas with your mama and sister?" said Lula.

"Went without me. Took 'em a bus to Houston's what I hear. Ain't heard more."

Beany and Lula looked at each other, then Beany said, "Why don't you come in with us, Eclair? We'll figure out what to do for you after while. I'm Beany Thorn and my friend here is Lula Pace Fortune Ripley."

"Miz Beany?" Eclair said. "I be hoodooed."

"What's that?" asked Lula. "What you mean?"

"Hoodoo man name Cap'n Funeste spell me, lay a curse on my head, say I be dead soon. Just gon' fall down and die."

"Why would anyone put a curse on you, Eclair?" Lula asked.

"Didn't do him right, I guess," said the girl.

"Let's go in," said Beany, "sort this out."

Eclair Feu extended her long, skinny arms to the sides,

her body began to vibrate and her eyes rolled back in her head. She urinated on the sidewalk, stuck out her tongue and started to whirl. The child spun around several times before she stopped. Her eyes came back into place and stared blankly straight ahead for a few moments. Eclair then turned right and began walking rapidly away in the direction of Rampart Street.

"Eclair!" Beany shouted, but the girl kept walking.

Marnie Kowalski poked her head out of the upstairs window again.

"You ladies comin' in, or what?" she said.

"We're comin'," Beany answered.

"Like you said," Lula said to Beany, "everything looks normal."

30

I have been having some mighty disturbing dreams of late. Last night I had one where someone was following me or was with me and at first I couldnt see who it was and then it turned out to be Mamas old friend and suitor Johnnie Farragut the private detective. We were in a snowy place and I met a girl who was from Czechoslovakia she said lived with her parents in a big apartment with wind blowing through cracks in the walls and windows next to railroad tracks in a northern city. She took me to her home and Johnnie followed behind. In the dream I was much younger than I am now maybe in my 20s or 30s and Johnnie was just as he always was somewhere in between not young or old just shuffling along behind the way he did after Mama so many years. The girl wanted me to meet her parents who did not speak English they wanted me to help them they were afraid to leave the apartment. I dont know how or where I met their daughter on the street I guess. The parents were dressed like country people from the forests of Eastern Europe the mother with a big black shawl over her head and shoulders and father in a shabby gray suit jacket and pants over a stained dirty long underwear shirt he had a big mustache and four day beard. Finally I understood that they wanted me and Johnnie to take them to a boat going to Egypt but it wasnt really Egypt it was an even more ancient place Mesopotamia maybe. I wouldnt take their money it was very little anyway and Johnnie tried to explain to them we couldnt get them there. The parents got angry the woman was shouting at us and the girl said nothing so Johnnie and I had to run out of there into the snowy street. This Marnie Kowalski sure is a character as Mama would say a tough talker but a hell of a good woman I believe and Beany does too. She no sooner had gotten us fixed in the upper right rear apartment on the courtyard which is nice with a little fountain water comes out of the mouths of bluebirds than here come Pace who Marnie called right after Beany buzzed her. Hes looking good losing more hair on top and in back but in shape from working construction these last few months. Marnie and he are best buddies were lovers once upon a time and somehow come out of that with good feelings towards one another a small miracle. Sat us down to a good meal of gumbo and cornbread. Pace had to get back to the job he and his crew are doing in Gentilly Terrace for the famous Mexican Japanese artist Arturo Okazaki y Pintura rebuilding his studio Pace said the water went up eight feet wrecked forty years of the mans work. Hard to imagine losing so much in a sudden see your whole life float away like that. Beany and I are having a rest and will see Pace later tonight. Marnie Kowalski bakes cakes for a living along with renting out her apartments. She has a tattoo of a red scorpion on the back of her left hand I asked her why a red one and she said so nobody would ever mistake her for an easy woman.

31

Lula, Beany, and Pace were in Saint Wolfgang's Lounge on Iberville Street sipping snowflake rickeys, a concoction created by Saint Wolfgang's owner, Koomgang Lee, a thirty-five-year-old North Korean defector, which combined Koomgang Lee's version of white lightning with lime and Schweppes. The North Korean proprietor, who claimed to at one time have been a commander in Kim Jong-il's supreme personal service brigade, had named his establishment Saint Wolfgang's because he had opened it on Halloween, his favorite Western holiday, which also happens to be Saint Wolfgang's Day.

"I been comin' in here regular," Pace told the women, "since I run into Marnie again. She's pals with Koomgang Lee. Baked him the first birthday cake he ever had, bittersweet chocolate, Barbancourt rum, and pineapple."

Billie Holiday singing "I Didn't Know What Time It

Was" lingered in the air. Koomgang Lee, Pace explained, was besotted by American culture of the 1940s and '50s, and was a jazz fanatic. He encouraged patrons to smoke, providing gratis each table in the lounge a mahogany case containing only unfiltered cigarettes: Lucky Strikes, Pall Malls, Chesterfields, and Camels. His vision of America had been formed by the movies, the viewing of which was a secret pastime of the North Korean dictator's, and one Kim Jong-il often enjoyed sharing with his closest associates, including those preferred members of his supreme personal service.

"Koomgang told me he smuggled himself out of North Korea buried under a heap of stinking fish guts used as chum on a shark trawler. Made it across the Yellow Sea to Quingdao, China, then walked a thousand miles to Shanghai. He presented himself at the US consulate there and offered information about the North Korean nutjob leader and the North Korean military in return for a visa to the United States. Two years later he settled in New Orleans."

"Heck of a story," said Beany.

"Blessed be he that fleeth from the fear," said Lula.

"Amen," said Pace, holding up his glass.

Lula and Beany raised their glasses, too, and the trio imbibed their snowflake rickeys.

"Tomorrow I'll take you on a tour of the ghost lands,"

Pace told them. "That's what we've taken to callin' those parts of town mostly abandoned now."

"It makes me so sad thinkin' about all those people forced to relocate and can't get back," said Beany.

"Not much to come back to in lots of cases," said Lula.

"Read where a mess of black folks were airlifted to Utah," Beany said. "Any of 'em been heard from since?"

"I know a lot of people, white and black, don't intend on comin' back," Pace said. "Most went to Texas, Houston in particular."

Lula nodded. "We met a young girl right when we arrived told us she got separated from her mama and sister who she figures got taken to Houston."

"Crime rate there's tripled, Kinky Friedman says," said Pace. "Blames it on exiles from N.O."

"He the Jewboy run for governor of Texas?" asked Beany.

"Exactly. Had a rock group called the Texas Jewboys. Writes mysteries, too. I read a few, they aren't bad."

"Talented fella," said Lula.

"Ready for another snowflake?" Pace asked.

"Not me, son. Beany, how 'bout you?"

"Seein' as how I ain't drivin' and I'm three and three-quarters past twenty-one, why not?"

Pace was about to signal for a waitress when Koomgang Lee himself came over to their table. He shook Pace's hand.

"How remarkably gracious of you to stop in this evening, Mr. Ripley," said Koomgang Lee. "Is everything to your satisfaction?"

"Absolutely, Koomgang. I'd like you to meet my mother, Lula, and her good friend, Beany. They just come in from North Carolina."

Koomgang smiled and nodded to the women. He wore his jet black hair combed straight back and was clean-shaven except for a dyed purple soul patch. His jaguar-like smile revealed even rows of very small teeth the color of balsa wood. He was wearing a gray sharkskin suit and a silver chainmail tee shirt. A Star of David hung from a gold chain around his neck.

"So pleasing to have you here in my home," he said to them. He sat down in a chair at their table.

"Pace," said Beany, "you didn't tell us Mr. Lee was such a sharp cat. Not tall but cute as hell."

"I was savin' the best for last just for your sake, Beany," Pace said. "I gave 'em the short version of your comin' to America, Koomgang."

"I have been reborn here, as you say," said the proprietor. "Now I am doing all I can to help rebuild those parts of this city that were mutilated so severely by the flood. People here have been so good to me, I am thankful for the opportunity to return the favor."

"Koomgang brought in a group of investors from Singapore to construct a new hospital," said Pace.

"You certainly are well-spoken, Mr. Lee," said Lula. "Did you know our language before you came here?"

"I knew only Korean and Mandarin until I found passage from Shanghai to Baltimore on an Israeli merchant ship. The crew of the *Altalena* taught me my first words in English and in Hebrew."

"Koomgang's converted to Judaism," Pace said.

Koomgang Lee laughed gently and fingered his soul patch. "Not precisely converted," he said. "Before, I was an atheist. The only belief system permitted in North Korea is the cult of the leader, Kim Jong-il. Now I am Reform Jew."

"I tried reformin' myself many times," said Beany, "but nothin' ever took for keeps. I guess I'm doomed to die apostate."

"This word you employ—apostate—" said Koomgang Lee, "is one I do not know."

"Means I got no faith. Nothin' in particular, anyway."

"To believe in yourself and in your duty to mankind is faith enough, Mrs. Beany."

"Miss Beany to you, Mr. Lee."

Koomgang Lee smiled without showing his tiny teeth, then stood up.

"It has been a most highly remarkable pleasure to have

made your acquaintances and to talk with you," he said to the ladies. "Will you be in New Orleans for long?"

"Not very, I don't think," said Lula.

"But we'll be sure to come back in here before we go," said Beany.

"Please do. Good to see you, Mr. Ripley, as always."

Pace and Koomgang Lee shook hands again before the owner moved to another table to greet his customers.

Count Basie and his orchestra played as Helen Humes sang "Between the Devil and the Deep Blue Sea."

"Maybe I will have another snowflake, son," said Lula. "I'm beginnin' to feel better about bein' back in N.O."

32

It was spooky driving around today with Pace. NO definitely aint the same place as I left it eighteen years ago. Sailors and my old house in Metairie is okay there wasnt much damage in Jefferson Parish but just about every neighborhood east got hit pretty bad except for high ground like the Quarter and the Marigny and parts of Uptown. Mounds of trash no stoplights or power drug dealers cruising around in cars Pace told me in the Lower Nine and New Orleans East dead bodies are being dumped and nobody does nothing about it. Ghost lands is a accurate description of those places. The tourist area is back up plenty of people carrying on on Bourbon so youd think nothing so terrible ever happened. When I lived here I dont think I was on that street six times in the last ten years or more. Now at Marnies Im two blocks away but still cant feature going anywhere near it other than maybe if we go to Galatoires I do miss their remoulade sauce I never tasted none better. Pace and his crew are working on Arturo Okazaki y Pinturas house and when they finish it will start repairing a restaurant out on Canal across from the high school Lee Harvey Oswald went to. Pace says there is enough work for him in and around NO to last him until he decides to retire and from what we saw of the devastation I cant disagree. Most of the workers are from Mexico not many from here which is a fact that troubles me. I would think that its the local inhabitants who could use the jobs there are plenty and the money. They cant all have gone to Houston. Marnie Kowalski has invited Beany and me to have dinner with her tonight shes cooking and wants us to meet her newest beau a movie director who is shooting a picture in Shreveport so hes only in NO on weekends. Marnie says hes famous his name is Doncovay Abidjan a half African who made a movie called Death Becomes You won prizes all over the world Marnie told us but neither Beany or me heard of it. Marnie says its about a young woman from a rich Boston family who falls in love with her husbands father whos the worlds leading expert on wasps she gets pregnant by him and they run off together to a made up South American country where he falls off a cliff trying to capture a wasp. She decides to stay there and live in this mountain village and have the child though she releases all the wasps her fatherinlaw kept to study and is stung in her eyes so she goes blind but has the baby who is a boy who grows up to become the leader of a revolution and then is president of the country. Before his mother dies she tells him her last wish is for her corpse to be thrown off the same cliff his father fell from and he honors her wish and years later she is made a saint who becomes the icon of a cult that each year several of its followers jump off this cliff to prove their devotion. Her son the president tries to break up the cult but he fails when members of the cult assassinate him and they take over the government. Beany said she didnt think shed like the movie I dont think I would either but I didnt say it to Marnie.

33

"*Mama,* this place out here's my own special pro bono project. Man owns it lived here thirty-nine years, lost his house and all his most prized earthly possessions but one. Wanted to show you now so when it's transformed into what I got in my head you'll say, 'My land, Pace Roscoe, I just wish your daddy was here to witness what a marvelous thing you gone and done.' What I love about you, Mama, nobody but you ever calls me by my fore-names."

Pace and Lula were rolling in Pace's red Dodge Ram east on St. Bernard Highway. He'd picked up his mother that overcast afternoon, leaving Beany and Marnie in deep discussion about the difference between clitoral and vaginal orgasms, the latter of which the eternally inquisitive Miss Thorn, even at her advanced age, remained unconvinced were anything more than an oriental myth.

"What's this man's name whose house you're gonna build for nothin'?"

"Luther Byu-Lee, Mama. Half Vietnamese, half black. His daddy was a cook on a Chinese freighter and his mama was a dancer at Big Dorothy's Shoo-Fly Club. Remember it? On Conti?"

Lula shook her head.

"Burned down, Luther told me. Anyway, he's a musician, one of N.O.'s best. Plays a dozen instruments but mostly alto sax. His horn's all he took with him when he escaped the flood."

"Sailor Ripley was partial to Charlie Parker. Said Bird took up alto 'cause Prez and Bean had a lock on tenor."

"Didn't know Daddy paid such close attention to jazz. Always thought he was more an old rock 'n' roll and R and B man."

"Sail listened to ever'thin', Pace, even classical. In his declinin' years, he got into a Hungarian composer, said his music made him feel like centipedes was slitherin' through his veins."

"Probably Bela Bartok," said Pace. "Charlie Parker liked his music, too."

Pace turned off onto a road strewn with everything from fallen trees to misshapen couches and rusted water heaters.

"Mr. Byu-Lee's meetin' us, Mama. There he is."

Seated on a wooden folding chair in the middle of a clean-swept plot of land was a large, burnt orange-colored, middle-aged man wearing a white shirt and brown slacks held up by red suspenders. He was playing a golden horn that glowed under the cloudy sky. Pace stopped his truck and cut the engine.

As they sat and listened, a nail of sunlight pierced the gray. After a minute, Lula said, "Lord in heaven, no Frenchman ever painted a prettier picture."

34

"*So* tell us, Mr. Abidjan," said Beany, "what's it like to hobnob with all them movie stars? Lula here had her an adventure once with a director."

"Oh, who was that?" asked Doncovay Abidjan.

"Man named Phil Reál," said Lula, "but it was ages ago."

"Of course," Abidjan said, "he made *Mumblemouth*, a classic in the horror genre."

"That was him," said Lula.

"It's a pity that he died before he could make *The Cry of the Mute*," said the director. "It is a legendary project. Those who were fortunate enough to have read the screenplay said that it was certain to have been his masterpiece."

Lula, Beany, Marnie, and Doncovay Abidjan were each on their second glass of champagne prior to having dinner in Marnie's house. Abidjan was a short, stout, coffee-colored man with heavy black-rimmed glasses and a goatee. He was wearing a bright yellow dashiki, a mauve scarf and a large pendant around his neck that represented the signs of the zodiac. Marnie Kowalski had told Lula and Beany before Abidjan arrived that he was a devout believer in astrology. "He's a Libra," Marnie had said, "he'll be nice to both of you."

"Actors are still children," the director said in answer to Beany's request. He laughed, sniffled briefly and continued, "Most of them have an emotional age of not more than fourteen, so, as a director, I treat them accordingly. I make them feel as though there is no other person on the planet who could do for me what I am asking, and sometimes this is even the truth."

"Surely not all of 'em are cases of arrested development," said Lula. "There must be some exceptions."

"There are," said Abidjan, "and those few I don't have to consider, they know what to do and how to do it. It is always a pleasure to have someone who shows up on time and has prepared him or herself sufficiently."

"Give us some examples," said Beany. "What about Eddie Epps? He's my fave these days. You ever worked with him?"

"Yes, on *Way Down in Egypt Land*."

"I saw it!" Beany said. "One where Eddie Epps is disguised as a French anthropologist but he's really Prince Balkanski of

Moldavia who's kidnapped and sold into slavery to a tribe of Nomads when he's explorin' the Sahara desert."

"It was the Gobi desert, actually," said Abidjan.

"He looked wicked cute in a burnoose. I loved the scene where the teenage girl with the bee lips who's also a slave really licks his wounds with her tongue. It's somethin' people always say meanin' not actually doin' it but she does it like I never seen before. Was that your idea, Mr. Abidjan, or was it in the script?"

"As the Arabs say, it was written."

"The writer never gets enough credit," said Lula. "That's what Sailor used to say."

"It's true," Marnie added. "Doncovay says the actors think they made up their lines all by themselves."

"No," said Abidjan, "what I said is that many of them believe they are spontaneously saying these words, not inventing but being."

"What's Eddie Epps really like?" asked Beany. "Is he as smart as he is cute?"

"Eddie is a delightful boy, when he wants to be. Now that he is married and a father, he seems calmer. His days of destroying hotel rooms and punching photographers are past, I think. His biggest problem now is controlling his weight. Between films he balloons up. He is addicted to *la cuisine rapide*."

"What's that?" Lula asked.

"Fast food," said Marnie.

"I will tell you a secret," said Abidjan. "Twice Eddie has had the liposuction."

"No!" Beany yelped.

"*Mais, oui.* The first time was before *Way Down in Egypt Land*, when he was only twenty-six. *C'etait necessaire* for the very scene you mentioned, Madame Beany, of the licking of the wounds."

"My land," said Lula, "who would have thought it?"

"This kinda thing is pretty common," said Marnie. "Doncovay's told me a whole hell of a lot of really nasty stuff. Some of it's downright creepy."

"Tell us somethin' creepy," said Beany, as she helped herself to another glass of champagne.

"Not before dinner," said Lula.

"Better before than after," said Beany. "Just a quickie."

"Tell 'em about Brenda du Sossé," said Marnie. "What happened with her and Federico Cazzissimo, the Italian producer."

"Brenda du Sossé, the old model?" Beany asked. "She's on those four A.M. infomercials now hawkin' Swiss face cream supposed to contain Miura bull semen. They make a big deal out of sayin' how no bulls are harmed durin' the process of obtainin' it."

"Go on, Doncovay, tell 'em," Marnie said. "Then we'll eat." The director took a swig of champagne, then began. "Everyone in the business knows how crazy this Cazzissimo is, how he would do anything to get what he wants. He owns television stations, newspapers, ships, everything, grocery stores in Nepal, you name it. Money means everything and nothing to him. So, when Brenda du Sossé was at the height of her fame, twenty years ago, when she was often referred to as the most beautiful woman in the world, Federico Cazzissimo pursued her tirelessly. He offered to marry her many times but she refused. She told him it was not because he was so ugly—which he still is, he resembles a buzzard with two necks—but that in order for her to have a vaginal orgasm, the man's cock must, when fully erect, to measure at least nine and one-half inches. Cazzissimo's member, apparently, while of normal proportions, fell well short of her requirement."

"Marnie," said Lula, "let me have a little bit more of that champagne."

"The Italian producer," Abidjan continued, "located an Austrian surgeon who claimed that he could construct from a cadaver a super penis and transplant it onto Federico Cazzissimo's body."

"This really happened?" asked Beany. "How could he connect the nerve endin's and everything?"

"Hush, Beany," said Lula.

"The doctor—I forget his name, he's dead now—"

"Committed suicide," said Marnie, "after he was exposed as a Nazi experimented on prisoners in concentration camps durin' World War II."

"—assured Cazzissimo that the surgery would be successful, the first of its kind. Federico promised him that if the transplant worked, he would personally endorse the procedure and make the doctor wealthy beyond his wildest dreams. Cazzissimo swore that he could arrange for the doctor to be awarded the Nobel Prize for medicine.

"The operation was performed and several months later, after, as you say, the kinks had been worked out and he was completely healed, the producer made a rendezvous with Brenda du Sossé."

"Did he produce?" asked Lula. "Sorry, I just had to say it."

"He did," said Abidjan, "but Brenda du Sossé, impressed as she must have been, insisted on measuring his member. She got down on her knees and did so. According to the tape, Cazzissimo's member in full erection came—no pun intended—to precisely eight and five-eighths inches, and she declared it insufficient for her purposes. *Quel dommage*, almost but not quite. Enraged by her rejection and seized by uncontrollable desire, Federico Cazzissimo forcibly introduced his cadaver-derived organ into Brenda du Sossé's mouth."

"And she bit it off!" Beany exclaimed.

Doncovay Abidjan nodded, and said, "Only the engorged head. He was flown as soon as possible in his private jet, with the may I say, decapitated part packed in ice, from Paris, where he and Brenda du Sossé had had their rendezvous, to the mountainside clinic in Austria, so that the surgeon could reattach it."

"Could he?" Lula asked. She felt like she had as a little girl listening to *The Wolves of Willoughby Chase* on the radio.

"Evidently, yes," said Abidjan, "but in any case that was the *dénouement* of Cazzissimo's quest for the favors of Brenda du Sossé. One year later, he married a Sicilian barmaid."

"Did they have children?" asked Lula.

"This is the best part," said Marnie.

"Five," said Abidjan.

"No!" gasped Beany.

"*Oui*," Abidjan said, "but four were by artificial insemination."

"And the other one?" Beany asked.

"Who knows?"

"You ladies are gonna love this," said Marnie, as she got

up and headed for the kitchen. "I got us some mighty tasty boudin sausages for supper."

35

Lula and Marnie were sitting in Marnie's kitchen having their morning coffee and Marnie had just lit up her first American Spirit of the day when they heard Beany shout in the front room. Lula got up and went in and saw her friend hang up the telephone. There was no phone in their apartment and they had come to Marnie's, at her invitation, so that Beany could call Hedy Lamarr.

"It's Melton," said Beany, "he went postal."

Marnie came in, carrying her cup and cigarette.

"Can you spare me one of them?" Beany asked.

Marnie handed her cigarette to Beany, who accepted it and took a big drag.

"What's up?" asked Marnie.

Beany puffed away. Her eyes were full of tears that refused to fall or that she refused to allow to fall. Lula had seen her this way before, "caught between brawlin' and bawlin'," as Beany described herself when in this state.

"Somethin' happened to her grandson, Melton," Lula told Marnie.

"Not 'to,'" said Beany, "it's what he done."

Beany inhaled on Marnie's American Spirit until it was almost down to the filter. Lula and Marnie waited and watched her smoke.

"He murdered Delivery," Beany said. "Shot his own daddy with a deer rifle."

"Hell's bells!" Lula cried. "You talk to Hedy?"

"Even a child is known by his doings," said Marnie, "whether his work be pure, and whether it be right."

Beany handed what was left of the cigarette back to Marnie and said, "Hedy Lamarr says Delivery was eatin' his breakfast as usual, four eggs sunnyside up, six pieces of Canadian Bacon, and five slices of raisin walnut toast, when Melton just come marchin' out of his room bare naked, carryin' the gun. Hedy Lamarr was standin' by the stove, she says. Delivery didn't even know his son had come in until he touched the barrel end against the back of his daddy's head and pulled the trigger. Delivery's brains spewed out onto his plate, turned the eggs red."

"He didn't shoot at Hedy, did he?" asked Lula.

Beany shook her head. "Melton turned right around and walked back calmly to his bedroom and closed the door. The police just come and taken him into custody. Hedy Lamarr says he didn't give 'em no trouble. Had guns drawn and bulletproof vests on like it was Scarface they was after."

"He say anything to them?"

"Not to the cops, to his mama. As he was bein' hauled away, he said, 'As long as he is a child differeth nothin' from a servant, though he be lord of all.'"

Marnie walked out of the room. Lula went over and sat down next to Beany and held her close. Marnie came back with two more cigarettes, put both between her lips, lit them, and handed one to Beany.

"I guess we'll be movin' on to Plain Dealin' sooner than expected," Lula said to Marnie. "I'm sure Hedy Lamarr's in dire need of her mama."

"He never forgave his father for bein' a midget," said Beany. "For makin' a son who was a midget, too."

Marnie looked out the front window at the sky. Fast moving clouds headed toward the Gulf of Mexico.

"We're in for some weather," she said.

36

"*Really*, Lula, you don't have to cut short your visit. You ain't hardly had no time with Pace."

"I'm comin', don't argue. Pace understands, he promised he'll visit real soon. I won't let you face this mess without me."

Lula and Beany had said their goodbyes to Marnie and Pace and were sitting in Lula's Mercury Nightcat, Lula at the wheel.

"Don't think I don't appreciate it," Beany said. "If I could love you any more for it than I already do, I would. I'm sure Hedy Lamarr'll want you there. Spike Jones and Tizane Naureen drove on up together last night."

Lula started the car, made certain nobody was coming and pulled out of her parking space.

"What about Elmo?"

"Tizane Naureen called the nursin' home in Ferriday, but

you know he's been gaga for the last few years. Nurse there said she'd tell him but doubted he'd understand."

"Why's he in Ferriday, anyway? Isn't that where Jerry Lee Lewis is from?"

"Yes, it is, birthplace of The Killer himself, though I believe he's lived over in Hernando, Miss'ippi, for decades. Elmo's last wife, Nefertiti Larto, was from near there. She passed last year. They'd been livin' in Sicily Island until Elmo got the Alzheimer's so fierce nobody could handle him at home."

"Life just don't quit, Miss Thorn, does it?"

"You quit life, it don't quit you, is how I see it. By the way, Spike Jones says it'll be his pleasure to carry you back to Bay St. Clement, so don't worry none on that score."

"I ain't been worryin', but thanks. How's Hedy Lamarr doin' today?"

"Holdin' steady at the moment, far's I can tell. Nothin' to be done about her husband, he's gone, so her concern's for the boy. Says their lawyer thinks there won't be no trial, just a hearin' to determine Melton's mental condition. Lawyer believes he'll be declared a deranged individual and spend the rest of his days in the bin. It ain't no fun, I know, 'cause I been more'n once, but better that than Angola. Hard cases in there'd be usin' his bones for toothpicks."

They had decided to take the interstate out of N.O. to

Baton Rouge, then the 190 to highway 71, which would take them almost all the way to Plain Dealing. The last stretch, from Bossier City north on highway 3, Beany said, was no more than twenty miles.

Lula reached for the radio, then asked, "You mind?"

"'Course not, baby."

Lula cut on the dial and there was old Jimmy Reed again, singing one of Sailor's favorite tunes, "Blue, Blue Water."

"You know I never loved before," he crooned, "and I don't want to love no more."

Lula turned to tell Beany "My feelings exactly," but her friend had fallen asleep as soon as they had turned off Elysian Fields onto the 10.

"Blue, blue water, silver moon, tell me, darlin', tell me soon," Lula sang along softly. Then she stopped singing and just listened as she drove.

37

Every time I been in Baton Rouge I recall Sailor telling me about how when he was a boy his daddy would take him to visit his grandmama and theyd spend a Sunday afternoon riding the old paddlewheeled ferryboats on the Mississippi River back and forth for hours between Baton Rouge and Port Allen eating Crackerjacks and drinking Delaware Punch. Also his daddy took him to look at the bullet holes still in the Capitol walls where the famous governor of Louisiana Huey P. Long was assassinated. He said Huey was a hero of his daddys and that if he had lived he might could have been president of the USA and changed things for the ordinary working man much better but Huey was shot down in cold blood and nobody would ever know. Beany and I have stopped at the Inn of Evangeline in Ville Platte for the night its Cajun country the people are always informal but polite which I like. Beany been more quiet than normal not talking a mile a minute the way she does. This business has hit her hard like a thief in the night snuck in and taken away her energy. All day driving I done my best to make conversation but Beanys down in the rock bottoms. We ordered in to the room from a chop suey joint rice and sweet and sour pork and snow peas but Beany only picked at it she never was too eager a eater anyway. One of the coins I got in change for the Chinese was a Indian head nickel with a buffalo on the tails side. I told Beany I had not seen one of these in so many years. When I was girl in grade school they were pretty common but by the time I was in high school they was becoming rare and I wrote a report about how it was the Indian head nickel came to be I still remember some of it. I always have thought the Indian face was very sad had hard crease lines in the right cheek and forehead it is his profile of course with only a couple of feathers not a full head dress. This coin was ordered to be made by President Teddy Roosevelt the Rough Rider he was called and the government produced them for 25 years from 1913 to 1938. This one I have is from 1937. The artist who drew it was James Earle Fraser he modeled it after three Indian chiefs they were Iron Tail a Oglala Sioux who fought beside Sitting Bull beat the pants off Custer and the 7th Cavalry at Little Big Horn and Two Moons he was a Cheyenne also was at Little Big Horn and

Big Tree who was a Seneca the most famous of the three he became a movie actor his real name was Isaac Johnny John. The only movies I recall now are Drums along the Mohawk and She Wore a Yellow Ribbon the first with Henry Fonda the second with John Duke Wayne in the one with John Wayne Big Trees name was Chief Pony That Walks I always liked that name. Its wild I still can remember writing about the nickel must be 65 years ago and also the buffalo used by the artist was from the Bronx Zoo in New York and its name was Black Diamond. Looking at the Indian face now he still seems sad as hell I imagine because his land and ways of life was destroyed by the coming of the white man and the black man too. In North Carolina there is the legend of the Trail of Tears with the Cherokees Johnny Cash played one in a TV movie about it. I always have thought the Indian tribes of the Great West were the most beautiful their blankets and clothes and body decorations riding paint ponies galloping into the sundown. The white man certainly did not do them no favors did they. Im going to keep this nickel and never spend it so I can look at his sad but beautiful face whenever I want to for the rest of my life it reminds me of the girl who I was when I wrote about him.

38

"*Don't* believe I ever told you about this, Lula, but one time I was in Shreveport, actually stayin' over in Dixie Gardens, guess it was, Elmo Pleasant had a bit of business there, prob'ly buyin' or sellin' stolen property of some kind, as usual, and I run into a gal from Mer Rouge, over by Bastrop, name of Vahida Doblez."

"Sounds like a Mexican movie star."

Beany had awakened in better spirits and insisted on driving. They had just bypassed Alexandria and Beany had been chattering practically nonstop since breakfast.

"Her daddy hailed from around Nacimiento, Mexico, she told me, part black, part Indian, and her mama was white, from El Paso, if I recall correctly. Anyway, Vahida was a real knockout, long black hair, big dark brown eyes, fabulous figure. We was both in our early thirties then. Vahida had a bad problem, though."

"Who don't?"

"She didn't have full control of her faculties. Used to she'd pass out at the drop of a hat, any time, any place. Boom! One second she'd be standin' and carryin' on normal, next she's in a heap like a pile of rags."

"What was it? Epilepsy?"

"No, just faintin' spells. Doctors couldn't figure out why she had 'em. Sometimes she'd wake up and not know who or where she was."

"Amnesia."

"Said her mem'ry'd disappear for hours, even days."

"How'd you meet her?"

"We was stayin' at the same motel, hangin' out by the pool with our kids. She had one, I already had Hedy Lamarr. Her old man was in plumbin' parts. Vahida and I hit it off and we went together one evenin' into Shreveport, left the children with their daddies. Had us a few cocktails in a nice restaurant, sittin' at the bar makin' girl talk, when a couple swingin' dicks in suits begin hittin' on us, 'specially on Vahida. I was polite and all but didn't need no more company, made that clear. Vahida Doblez, though, didn't mind the attention at all. She had on a tight-fittin', strapless, tangerine-colored dress didn't leave a whole lot to any man's imagination. Recall I tried to get her to leave but Vahida let the men buy us another round or two. She drank

Maker's Mark, on the rocks, nothin' fancy. I knew if we kept on we'd be cruisin' for a bruisin' but Vahida was drivin'. Only way out of it for me was to take a cab. I didn't want to leave her there with those two guys. Said they was pharmaceutical salesmen from Wichita, someplace like that. I'd told Elmo we wouldn't be late and Vahida said for me to go on, she'd be along soon."

"Don't tell me. You left her and she passed out."

Beany nodded. "That's what Vahida said two days later when the New Orleans police contacted her husband, whose name I forget. He and their little boy were still at the motel, tryin' to find out what happened to her."

It started to rain again, so the women rolled up the windows and Lula turned on the air-conditioning.

"Them big black cumulo-nimbus clouds're guardin' heaven's gate like Nubian eunuchs blockin' the door to Cleopatra's boudoir," said Beany.

"What did happen?" Lula asked.

"Manager of the Monteleone Hotel called the cops when a maid found Vahida unconscious and naked in a bathtub half-filled with dirty water. She didn't remember nothin', of course, once the hotel doctor revived her. Vahida's purse and clothes was there but no men. Night clerk said she'd come in with a man who'd apparently given a false name and address and paid for the room with cash in advance. Her car was found right where we'd left it, in the parking lot of the restaurant in Shreveport.

"How'd you find out?"

"Had her home number in Mer Rouge. Got hold of her husband there about a week later. He had the red-ass at me for abandonin' Vahida, as he called it, but turned out she was unharmed, except for the tattoo."

"Now there's a detail," said Lula. "Vahida's husband tell you this?"

"No, she did when I spoke to her the day after I talked to him."

"What was it?"

"Three letters: A, G, and M, inside a heart."

"Man's initials, prob'ly."

"Most likely, but it weren't the tattoo so much upset her husband, it was the location."

There was a thunderclap, then Beany said, "It was smack on Vahida's butt."

Lula clucked her tongue. "How much longer their marriage last?"

"Don't know, never spoke to Vahida Doblez again. She said she'd call back but she didn't, so I let it be."

"Couldn'ta been a happy husband havin' to look at another man's initials on his wife's ass every night."

"A stranger's at that."

Rain came down harder and Beany switched the wipers to high.

"Stop up at the next exit, Beany, will you? Water streamin' down like this always makes me want to pee."

39

Tizane Naureen and Spike Jones are real good kids they been regular to see Melton in the hoosegow and the situation pretty much seems to be as Beany been told looks like a verdict of insane will keep Melton in a institution for the criminal insane the duration of his days. Hedy Lamarr wont never be entirely all right again I dont guess but she and Beany is close now its a big help they werent always on such good terms. I was sorry to have to leave Pace so sudden but Beany needed me and there werent no question about it. Maybe instead of going straight to Bay St. Clement Ill ask Spike Jones to accompany me back to NO or Ill tell Pace to come visit here so he wont have to make a long trip to North Carolina and take more time away from his construction work. I been thinking on this business of fathers and sons and why Melton felt he needed to murder his own daddy. Beany says when she visited Melton at the jail he was real calm and didnt seem sad or happy just peaceful. I asked Hedy Lamarr if her boy been drugged stupid to keep him under control and she said she didnt think so as he had not given the authorities any trouble at all since they took him away. Pace and Sailor always got along good even when Pace got into trouble I think because Sail himself had hard times coming up and then later of course so he tried to keep things together for our family and he did he took care of us. Sailor and Pace never known I found out about the time Pace hooked up with them two nasty Rattler brothers when he was sixteen and got involved in a robbery and then those boys were killed over in Mississippi and Sailor had to rescue his son while I was away in Rock Hill with the church of the three Rs when Reverend Goodin Plenty was shot to death in front of my eyes. I never have said a word to Pace in all this time and wont ever and not to Sail while he was alive that was their trial by fire not mine. As John says the father loveth the son and hath given all things into his hand. I know how very much Sailor loved Pace and did his best to keep him right. Despite its terrible what Melton done to his daddy the pain of the son hath delivered Delivery from the burden of Babylon. I remember when I was nine or ten years old hearing about a orphanage fire in a big city up north where the children were crowded on the stairs trying to get out of the building when the staircase collapsed and all of the children were crushed and burnt up. The staircase made of cement was not strong enough to support the weight of those kids it was supposed to be but wasnt built properly the construction company had cheated on the grade of cement or something to save money the result being those orphans were killed. I thought how lucky I was to not be an orphan have to get trapped in a fire like that. Jesus said suffer little children and forbid them not to come unto me for such is the kingdom of heaven. What about a forever boy like Melton not right in his brain what happens to him? I am ready for an answer why theres endless madness and suffering on the planet all I know is everything been out of control from the beginning.

40

Beany and Hedy Lamarr were on their way back to the house after visiting Melton when Hedy's cell phone rang. She was driving but took the call anyway.

"Hedy Lamarr here. Oh, hi, Spike, we're just now startin' home. What? That can't be! Oh, Lord, give us strength. Of course, Mama and I'll head there right now."

Hedy Lamarr ended the call and moved her Durango over into the far right lane, then turned right onto Confederate Highway.

"What're you doin', darlin'?" asked Beany. "You need to make a stop?"

"Yes, Mama. I got to tell you this, so be calm, okay?"

"Now that you got me nervous, I'll do my best. What is it?"

"Lula's in the hospital. She's breathin' but won't wake up. Tizane Naureen and Spike Jones are with her at Marshall Clements Memorial. We'll be there in ten minutes."

Beany sat perfectly still and stared straight ahead. She did not want to believe what her daughter had just told her. Beany wanted to go back in time fifty-seven seconds to before Spike Jones had called his mother. The thought of Lula passing away was not one for which Beany was prepared.

"Kids say doctor told 'em it's possible Lula had a stroke while she was nappin', now she's in a coma."

"Anybody call Pace?"

"I don't know, Mama. We can do it from Marshall Clements."

The image of Lula Pace Fortune at twenty popped into Beany's head. The night before Sailor Ripley was released from prison for killing Bob Ray Lemon, she and Lula had gone to the Raindrop Club in Cape Fear to talk and try to soothe Lula's nerves; Lula did not know what to expect when she picked up Sailor the next morning at Pee Dee. Lula had long, wavy, black hair then, and her big gray eyes made a person staring into them think of a midsummer's day sky just before rain. Now those cool, late afternoon eyes were closed, possibly for keeps, and the thought gave Beany the shivers.

Hedy Lamarr said, "Spike Jones told me his shrink, Ramar Rabinowitz, who's half-Jew and half-Pakistani, says Tibetans believe if a sick or hurt person lives or dies, it don't matter, they're both good."

A gigantic bug banged against the windshield, leaving a greenish-yellow squish mark directly in Beany's line of vision, but neither she nor Hedy Lamarr said another word until they arrived at the hospital.

41

Sailor took Lula's hand in his.

"Thanks for waitin', Sail," Lula said.

"Peanut," said Sailor, "don't give it another thought."

CODA

Dear Pace,

As upsetting as it is we got no choice but to accept the fact of your Mamas passing. I am not certain she is in a better place this is only my thought not based on nothing but face it there aint nothing can be proved even by science concerning an afterlife. I heard today on the radio that astronomers have dug up a old idea of Albert Einsteins called dark energy they now believe might be true after all even though Einstein had decided it was his biggest mistake. This is a force in space he figured was a ugly form of gravity he named a cosmological constant to explain a balance between the expansion of the universe and how certain stars are yanking on everything causing all there is around us to expand and dark energy is this invisible force. Believe it or not Pace I always was interested in this type of thinking as I never have believed in God creating it all. I mean there has to be a better answer thats too easy as is the big bang. Lula was my dearest friend more than a sister for almost all our lives and I considered her a powerful force of love which is the biggest mystery after all how she could keep on the way she did being good and thoughtful of others without getting fooled too much. Now the dark energy come pulled her away from us and I dont mean Satan who is only an excuse exists in stupid peoples minds. Lulas soul is swirling in space part of the expansion of the universe which is bigger for her having been and being.

Love you,
Beany

THE TRUTH IS IN THE WORK

Barry Gifford in conversation with Noel King

BERKELEY, CALIFORNIA, JUNE 27, 2007

NOEL KING: You have lived in San Francisco for a long time, while also having spent considerable time in London, Paris, and Rome, and your memoir writing recalls an early childhood of traveling, hotel rooms, moving from Chicago to Florida. What drew you to San Francisco and what changes have you observed during your years living here?

BARRY GIFFORD: I originally came out here to get a ship. That was January 1967. I was working as a merchant seaman and had been living in Europe for quite a while, since 1965, in London and Paris, working on ships, and then I came out here because I wanted to go to the Far East. And January 1967 was an amazing time to come here, so I stayed for five months and then went back to Europe, to London and Paris again, and came back in January 1968 and knew that I wanted, at least for a while, to base myself here, because I knew that I liked San Francisco. In those days it wasn't crowded, it was cheap, and beautiful, very Mediterranean, very European at that stage, with a very liberal atmosphere. And one other important thing about first coming to San Francisco, I really felt that Asian connection, it's one aspect I always enjoy here. So all those things added up. Plus there was a very rich labor history, and literary history, and I loved the climate. Low humidity, no bugs! All those things contributed to it.

Then I met a girl here and started a family and so my kids were all born here and have grown up in San Francisco, and I've used it as a base ever since. I've lived in other places, in Rome and Paris, I spend a lot of time in New York, and of course I go wherever I need to be for work. Yet I'm always happy when I come back here. So San Francisco has changed insofar as it's become overcrowded and much more expensive, like most places. But most of my kids are around, there are grandchildren now, and, basically, if you're "grandfathered in," the way I am, it still suits me, so it's still the most comfortable place for me to be based.

NK: I have read that you had a relationship with an Italian actress and spent a few years dividing your time between the US and Italy.

BG: I spent four years travelling between here and Rome but that ended ten days before 9/11. I came back here for my oldest boy's wedding and didn't go back. But I hadn't intended to go back, I was ending that period of my life.

NK: Your writing makes easy reference to several other languages and cultures, most obviously French and Mexican. Which languages other than English are you most familiar with?

BG: Well, as my old friend Daniel Schmid, a Swiss director, once said, "I speak six languages, all imperfectly!" In my case I can't say I'm fluent in any language other than English but I do speak some Spanish, French, Italian, even some Japanese. The thing is that when I go to a place and spend some time there, I make the effort. And look, language is what I work with. I have a pretty good ear and even if my vocabulary isn't always as extensive as it should be, or as I would like it to be, I've often been complimented by native speakers on my accent, and that's just because I listen.

When I get into something, I tend to go to the end of it. When I came back here from Europe I started going to Mexico a lot, spending a lot of time in Mexico City and Veracruz. It was closer than Europe, it was a little bit easier. And I still go wherever I need to go for my work, that's the nature of the business.

NK: How did your *Bordertown* photo-book collaboration with David Perry come about?

BG: *Bordertown* was a great project because an editor then at Chronicle Books in San Francisco—who were doing beautiful visual and photo books—came to me and offered me a great deal, and said we'll pay you to go wherever you want and you choose the photographer. I chose to do a photo and text book, which I'd never done, and I chose to spend the time on the US/Mexico border. At that time I was writing a lot about the border; I'd written *59 Degrees and Raining*, and that was made into a film, *Perdita Durango*, and I wrote *The Sinaloa Story*. I'd always been drawn to the area but I really wanted to explore it in more detail. And so David Perry, the photographer, and I spent quite a bit of time on the border, driving all over the place, and the result was *Bordertown*. And then a second book version was published, *The Four Queens*, in a very, very fancy, very expensive, limited edition by a San Francisco gallery, Gallery 16, for $1500 a crack, one of those things. *Bordertown* is a book I'm very proud of. It's won many awards, and I think David Perry is, since Robert Frank, one of the great black and white photographers of our time, underrated perhaps, and photography is a difficult business to be in. I don't know so much about it.

NK: Your website contains a documentary, available for viewing, called *Bordertown: A Journey with Barry Gifford* (Georges Luneau, France, 1999). That's where I learned the term "wetback" was initially applied to cattle before being applied to Mexicans wanting to move into the US, so it was a doubly offensive term.

BG: That was made for French television. Georges Luneau was the director, and again, we trawled along the border and reenacted some of those scenes, and went back to some of the places that David Perry and I had been, and some other places. The French and the Italians like to do these documentaries, like the Italian feature film, *Barry Gifford: Wild at Heart in New Orleans* (1999, 80 min.) which I really like. They like to put the writer in his milieu and since so much of my fiction has been set in New Orleans, that's why the Italians decided to use it as a background, pre-Katrina. I was actually just back there recently. The same is true of the French, they wanted me on the border because it's the setting for a lot of my fiction.

NK: They like putting the writer in his fictional situ, as a French TV company did when Matthieu Serveau made a film on (and with) Jim Crumley, *L'Esprit de la route* (France, 2002).

BG: Exactly.

NK: In *The Devil Thumbs a Ride and Other Unforgettable Films* (later reissued as *Out of the Past: Adventures in Film Noir*) you mention watching Robert Aldrich's film, *Autumn Leaves*, and connect it with your recollections of a time with your mother and one of her husbands, and you say that the song in that film was one of your mother's favorites, along with "La vie en rose." And your story, "The Ciné," from *Do the Blind Dream?* is a lovely playing out of a scenario involving a young boy, his father, and the movies. Leaving aside, for a moment, your extensive screenwriting, your fiction writing seems very connected to the history of cinema, with movie-going as a very important experience.

BG: First of all, when I was a child, my mother loved to go to the movies, especially foreign films, and she used to take me with her, all the time. So early on I was really inculcated with this love of cinema and an interest in the way people lived. And even if, as a very small child, I didn't understand necessarily what was going on at the movies, I retained the images in my head, and the dialogue. And I became interested in the way people spoke. Also, I was left alone a lot as a child, so I would stay up all night watching movies, and that's really where I developed my sense of narrative, and a very visual sense of how to tell a story. I think that's really where it began, and I've retained it ever since. I'd never really thought about it in terms of writing for the movies because that was not my initial orientation. I started by writing stories, and that was it, it was all about telling stories, and using my imagination, being free to do so, and it wasn't until much later that the movies came to me, basically. My novels began being bought for film, and then I began being asked to write for the movies.

Actually I was asked to write for film quite early on, right after my novel *Port Tropique* came out (1980). I wrote the screenplay for *Port Tropique*, which was deemed unacceptable for film. But it was better than the couple written subsequently by so-called professionals. I say that now because I re-read it again recently and I realize it's better than the other ones that were written. In any case, that movie never got made. So early on I was asked to spend some time in LA, in Hollywood, to write dialogue and to doctor scripts, and I turned it down. My children were really little and I wanted to be around here and have the time with them. The money didn't mean so much at that point, not that I didn't need the money, I absolutely needed it, but it just didn't seem right. I said, when I really do this, I want to come in the front door, and that's what finally happened a few years later.

NK: Your collaborations with David Lynch are celebrated and ongoing, and your piece on his *Blue Velvet* in your initial collection of essays on noir films, *The Devil Thumbs a Ride*, was slightly critical of that film.

BG: We've talked at various times about his work or my work, and I'm sure it came up but I don't think it was an offensive essay.

NK: Not at all.

BG: I was just telling my reaction to it. And I have to say something about that. That essay was written off the top of my head after seeing *Blue Velvet* the first time, and then when I saw it again later, a couple of times, I revised my opinion of it to some extent. My initial impression is still the same and that should never be tampered with. Lynch is so affecting. It's a tribute to David that he can so profoundly affect people through the use of images and sounds. Certainly my experiences with him have proved that. I saw him again just recently. I went to a screening of his recent film, *Inland Empire*. In any case, I love David and I love what he does.

NK: Well it's been a great collaboration across film (*Wild at Heart, Lost Highway*) and TV plays (The Hotel Room Trilogy, two of which, "Tricks" and "Blackout," Lynch directed). At the start of *The Devil Thumbs a Ride*, you say you imagined yourself in the situation of the 1950s *Cahiers du Cinéma* critics, writing at one a.m. in a café or at a kitchen table. You have some great, pizazzy moments of vivid description and re-narration in these essays, such as your description of the denouement of a scene in Jean Negulesco's *Roadhouse*, "It's the wigged out Widmark who takes the pipe." And Elmore Leonard said that many of your essays on these films were better than many of the films, and that is coming from a guy who would really like those films.

BG: Well, I'm a writer and it's always primarily the use of language. One thing that I'm always concerned with is the preservation of language. For example, when I wrote *Wyoming*—which was published on its own as a novel and now is included in *Memories from a Sinking Ship*, and which was also made into a play, which I adapted here for the Magic Theatre in San Francisco—I was really doing it to preserve the language of the period. The book is set in the early and mid-1950s in the Midwest and South of the United States but in fact the mother really is using a vernacular from the 1920s and 1930s. And I found that a lot of that language was disappearing, a lot of expressions, a lot of the manner of speech, all of that, and I really wanted to preserve it. And I did so by writing a whole little novel, if you will, in dialogue, except for one chapter, which is not included in *Memories from a Sinking Ship*, and a short film was made of that too, *Ball Lightning* (Amy Glazer, 2002), mentioned on the website. That's always been important, so I suppose the kind of writing that's done in my essays, as well as elsewhere, is always going to contain this element.

NK: Yes, that close attention to historical details of everyday speech, aspects of the quotidian.

BG: Correct. So I'm always trying to have the language relate to the detail of the time, of the film or whatever I'm writing about.

NK: You have been involved in the ongoing Francis Coppola *On the Road* film project. I read that you had suggested Gus Van Sant as a possible director. Is that project still happening, or is it lost in preproduction hell?

BG: Unfortunately, that has been the one biggest disappointment I have had in dealing with the movie business. Francis came to me and asked me to write the screenplay for *On the Road*. He'd had a number written before mine, and probably even after. I know that he and Michael Herr wrote one afterwards. Anyway, I wrote the screenplay, this must have been 1995 or so, and it was all set to go with Gus Van Sant directing, Francis producing. Everybody wanted to be in the movie, it was green-lit at Columbia Pictures, and then the deal fell apart due to Francis's own conflicts with Columbia Pictures over another deal.

And basically he took *On the Road* with him and so the movie was not made at that point. I know he's got another group of people working on it now, he's had several over the years, it's just too bad that we didn't get it done. I thought that really was an appropriate time, I thought Gus was the right director, completely, and Gus and I worked on the revisions together.

Anyway, that's what happened there. It was a privilege to be asked, and to work with Francis, and he told me that he liked my script very much. So did Columbia Pictures. So I did my part, but with a movie, you know, there are so many possibilities about things going wrong, more than go right, and the politics of it gets involved, and one thing and another. Maybe one day it'll get made.

NK: You have had a long involvement with all aspects of publishing, from small presses on the West Coast to big houses in New York, and your founding of Black Lizard Books. How did you initially come to connect with small press culture?

BG: I had a great introduction to this. My first book of poems was published in London. I was twenty, and when I came to San Francisco I was a poet basically, and I was introduced to printers, really fine letterpress printers. My first books in this country were done by a small press in Santa Barbara, Christopher's Books (run by Melissa Mytinger), and the books were printed by great printers like Graham McIntosh and Gary Albers. My first book of stories, *A Boy's Novel*, was done in letterpress, just amazingly beautiful. And I had friends here like Clifford Burke, Holbrook Teter, who were very famous letterpress printers. They worked for Andrew Hoyem and they would print broadsides, you know, poems on fine paper.

NK: Chapbooks!

BG: Yes, and so I really fell in love with printing itself, making fine press books. I had friends in New York who were also involved in this, so just seeing the word on the page, how it was arranged, how it was designed, how it was printed, all meant a lot to me. It was just this whole process of book-making—not the kind my father did (this said with a smile), but the actual printing of books—that interested me, and still does. So, small presses, such as they have been, have been very important to me and I just felt I needed to keep my hand in, with my books of poems or certain other chapbooks, things like *Read 'Em and Weep* (Dieselbooks, 2004) or *Brando Rides Alone* (North Atlantic Books, 2004), that I can redo later for inclusion in a larger collection to be published in New York or wherever. So I'm still into that. We might be at the end of the Gutenberg era, for lack of a better term, given the technological advances, if you want to call them that. I'm not, strictly speaking, a Luddite, but I think people are going to be missing a whole lot and in very short order. So I'm glad that I came in when I did, during the literary era, even the last stages of it perhaps. It's been a noble effort and I'm still interested in it.

So that was at the base of starting something like Black Lizard. Or even years before, back in the mid-1970s, when Gary Wilkie and I had a little press called The Working-man's Press, we published Allen Ginsberg and various other people in these sort of chapbooks, these small books. But everybody was doing that, everybody who was involved in the poetry world and all that. I was never really a part of the poetry world per se just as I'm not a part of any of these worlds really. I sort of have one foot in a bunch of them and just go where I want and do what interests me.

NK: On San Francisco and small presses, Paul Auster began out here with his first books of poetry and the initial individual volumes of his New York Trilogy, didn't he?

BG: Yeah, sure, Paul, who is an old friend of mine, began as a poet and a translator and we had a very similar arc, and then he got into movies later.

NK: To recall for a moment your Black Lizard publishing project (1984–1989) you must be happy to know that after falling through the cracks during the transition following the sale of Black Lizard titles, those already published and those commissioned, to Vintage/Random House, Elliot Chaze's *Black Wings Has My Angel* is now available as a print-on-demand title from BlackMask.com/Disruptive Publishing.

BG: I just cowrote a screenplay for it.

NK: I liked your essay about going to meet him, "Black Wings Had His Angel: A Brief Memoir of Elliot Chaze," originally published in *Oxford American* in 2000, and now available in your collection, *The Rooster Trapped in the Reptile Room.*

BG: I did meet Elliot Chaze, and his novel, *Black Wings Has My Angel,* was the last purchase I made for Black Lizard Books. Then, when Vintage/Random House took it over, they chose not to publish the book, much to my dismay, and to Elliot Chaze's dismay. And they blew it basically, because that was the quintessential Black Lizard book and I was sorry that they did not recognise that. But of course it's attained a semi-legendary status, partially due to my own efforts, and a producer in New York now holds the screen rights and, as I said, I just collaborated on the screenplay, so I hope they make the film. A film was made years ago by Jean-Pierre Mocky in France, *Il gèle en enfer* (1990). I never saw it but I heard it wasn't very good. Lynch and I wanted to do it. I had Lynch read the novel and he was all excited about it, but I couldn't get the rights. Elliot had sold the rights for $10,000 or something to Mocky. I don't blame him, he probably needed the money at the time. Anyway, it almost became a Lynch-Gifford film, it came very close, we would have done it.

NK: The range of your writing is very impressive. You write poetry, stories, novellas, novels, memoir, essays, biography, screenplays, and I see you have written a libretto and have a Japanese connection.

BG: In the early 1980s I was interviewed by a Chinese scholar who came to the US. He was writing a book for a publisher in Beijing, and he wanted to interview me about my poetry. He was interviewing various American poets whom he felt bore a relation to, and understanding of, the Chinese and Japanese poets throughout history and he came to interview me, which was nice. I had already been in Japan, I'd spent a couple of months there in 1975 but I'd always been drawn to the Asian poets, Li Po and Tu Fu, certainly, introduced by Ezra Pound and others. Then I really started reading Su T'ung-Po and Wang Wei, especially, in translation. I don't read Chinese, although I have studied Chinese written characters.

Then, years later, Toru Takemitsu, the Japanese composer, asked me to write a libretto for his opera, which became *Madrugada*, and was completed by Ichiro Nodaira after Toru passed away. And I thought Toru had asked me to do this because of *Wild at Heart*, the novel and the film, which was the most famous of my works, but he said, no, no, I ask you because of your poetry, your sensibility is close to mine, I'm a poet too. And I had not consciously recognised Takemitsu though I had heard his scores for dozens of films. He did ninety film scores, for Kurosawa (*Ran*, *Kagemusha*) and Teshigahara (*Woman of the Dunes*) and Philip Kaufman (*Rising Sun*), all that. So I knew his music in that sense but was ignorant of the fact that he had composed those scores. He was one of the most honored international composers, and I came to know him very well, and I was very flattered that he had approached me not because of my novels and films, but on the basis of my poetry. He knew of my relation to films and thought we could work together, and we did work well, and completed the libretto together. So I guess that Asian sensibility, or whatever else was the attraction to those poets, paid off.

NK: You have practiced in various forms and registers of writing that range from the avant garde to literary fiction to so-called genre writing. Have you noticed any difference in how your work is received in the US as opposed to Europe?

BG: The French don't seem to make much of a distinction between the two kinds of writing, though it was the editor

Marcel Duhamel who created the série noir at Gallimard, in 1945. If it makes it easier to classify in a bookstore or a library, fine, but I think we've seen crossover from so called genre fiction to literary fiction for so long now. I'm a literary writer but I've also worked as a journalist. Those category distinctions, that's for the academics to work out.

NK: When you start a new piece of writing, at what point do you know what genre it will be in—poem, novella, short story? In other interviews you've said you listen and wait for a voice to guide you.

BG: First off, it's great to have these various forms available to me to choose among. A thought occurs to me and it expresses itself, whatever the feeling or the story is. It might become a song. I still write songs. I came to poetry from song lyrics; or it might work better as a poem, a play, a novel, a story, or a film script. And sometimes it gets a little confusing, in that I might have chosen wrong in the beginning and I see that it will work better in another form and then I'll switch.

NK: What is an example of that?

BG: I started writing something that I thought might be a film treatment and then I realized that what I really wanted to do with it was a comic book, or I wanted it to be a graphic novel. So I started one called *Strange Cargo*, and now an illustrator is doing the drawings for it. There was a graphic novel made out of *Perdita Durango*, so it's possible, obviously, for an idea or a story to be exploited in more than one medium.

NK: And Auster's *City of Glass* was in that "Neon Lit" series, and another title came from the noir novel and film, *Nightmare Alley*.

BG: I loved Scott Gillis's drawings for *Perdita Durango*. I loved the artwork and I liked the presentation in Art Spiegelman's "Neon Lit" series. I think Auster has recently reprinted his graphic novel version of *City of Glass*, but I never reprinted *Perdita Durango* after that series stopped because I didn't like the script, which I did not do. Maybe I will reprint the book some day if I can get around to writing the script myself.

NK: On the matter of the film of *Perdita Durango* (Alex de la Iglesia, Spain/Mexico/US), I saw it on theatrical release in Sydney at the time of its first release and initial circulation and so I was surprised to read only a year or so ago in *Film Comment* that it was listed as one of their films "requiring a distributor." I had assumed that if I saw it in Australia on its original release, it certainly would have circulated theatrically here in the US.

BG: I wrote the first screenplay for it, I still get the lead screenplay credit, but unfortunately it was never given a theatrical release here. There were legal problems about product usage and images of Burt Lancaster and Gary Cooper and permissions hadn't been cleared.

NK: So they didn't have copyright for some territories?

BG: They were really stupid about that because it was supposed to be the film that made Javier Bardem a star here, and he did so well as Romeo Dolorosa. And of course Javier became a star anyway! He's a pal of mine, a wonderful guy, a great actor. Anyway, in the US *Perdita Durango* was only released on video, under a different title [*Dance with the Devil*], and some of the most important parts were cut out. So unless people go to see it at some special screening like at the Walter Reade Theatre in New York, or various repertory screenings, they can't see it. But they can get the UK DVD, which is a complete version of the film. I'm told the film was sold to the world and was released in at least forty countries.

NK: A friend of mine is a great fan of the film you cowrote with Matt Dillon, *City of Ghosts* (Matt Dillon, 2002). He really loves the music.

BG: That soundtrack is all Matt Dillon's work. He spent a great deal of time on it and I think it's a wonderful CD.

NK: Are you two likely to collaborate again?

BG: Yeah, we talk about it. I was just with Matt in New York and we're working on a new story, but it takes time getting together, getting our schedules straight, and then getting the money, but we've talked often about working together again.

NK: What is your daily writing regimen? When do you write, and what is your process for rewriting?

BG: Very early on I would write late at night, write any time, but after I started a family, I decided what I wanted was a more regular routine so I could sit down and have dinner with the family, with my kids. Of course the kids are all grown and gone now but I've maintained that same schedule, which is that I get up very early, and that's when I write, and I'm finished by one o'clock in the afternoon, and then I have the rest of the day. I think I'm certainly not alone in this, and it's worked out very well for me. But as years have gone on, of course, I'm interrupted more often and I have to avoid the telephone as much as possible, so I have an assistant who can take care of a lot of that, let alone emails and that sort of thing. I don't even have a computer.

NK: You have a typewriter there on your desk, covered by a tea-towel with a map of New Zealand on it.

BG: I still write in longhand, then I put it on the manual typewriter, then I give it to my assistant to put it on disk, so that's the process. And I find that writing early in the morning is still the best time for me. It's quiet, so I'm up by six o'clock still, virtually every day. That's my writing routine.

NK: Well, it worked for Hemingway, as you'd know. He'd write early, standing up, then go for his walk around Paris.

BG: My mind works the best in the morning. I know a lot of people who can't have a clear thought until noon, and that's fine, it depends on a person's rhythm, and what happens, but I have a very, very rich dream life and often the dreams carry over into my first waking hours, and somehow that transports me and puts me into that state where everything is suspended other than where I'm at in my writing mode. So if I'm working on a sustained piece, a novel, say, that's where I want to be, and I can't wait to be back there every day. But I also understand if I push it too hard, if I lean too hard on it, I can be wasting my time. I have to sort of follow that but stick with it. As Charlie Willeford told me many years ago, writing a novel is like building a house, every day you lay a few bricks, pretty soon you've got the house. And for lack of a better explanation that's pretty much how it works when you're doing something like that.

NK: So how does the process of rewriting work for you, as you move from a longhand version to manual typewriter to having someone put it on disk?

BG: Well, as I said, I write in longhand and when I go over what I've written in longhand I make changes, corrections, additions, so that's a second draft. Then I put it on a manual typewriter, so that's a third draft, and then I make corrections on that, so that's a fourth. Then I make a clean copy, so that's a fifth. So before it is put on disk there have been five drafts, and all very natural, and then I'll make further changes, not so extensively. There does sometimes come a time when at the point I'm ready to write, it's pretty much all there in my head. I just finished the seventh Sailor and Lula novella, *The Imagination of the Heart*, which will come out next year in the US and France. That's an example of a cohesive work that required very little revision.

NK: So it might come out in French first?

BG: I don't know if it will come out first in French [Éditions Rivages et Payot published the book in April 2009; Seven Stories Press in New York published it in May 2009] but the French are always on me for stuff. I publish fairly often in *La Nouvelle Revue Française*, and obviously all the Sailor and Lula stuff is very popular there, so it'll probably come out around the same time because it has to go through the process of translation. It's not very long. That's a sort of situation where I know these characters so well. I hadn't planned to go back to them, necessarily, but now Lula has her voice and she gets to tell her story her way, and she's eighty and it basically just flowed. I didn't have to revise it much at all, although I did revise it. That's the kind of thing where the voices are so familiar and the people are just talking. And my job is to get it down right.

NK: That sounds a bit like "the writer as amanuensis to the characters" idea. Tarantino once said he was like a court reporter when he got his characters talking . . .

BG: I don't mean to be disingenuous in this by saying I'm taking dictation. I'm creating, inventing and making all sorts of choices all along, but nevertheless Lula's is a very strong voice, and I know her intimately.

NK: Do you have a sense of which European and other literary cultures respond best to your work?

BG: Well, the Latin cultures respond very strongly and positively to my work. I had an email recently from a guy in Spain. I have a loyal readership in Spain, France, Italy, and Mexico. I don't know, maybe it's because some of my characters have Latin names, I'm not sure exactly why. Although some of my stories are set on the Mexico–US border. But I had this email recently from a guy who was a close friend of the Chilean writer, Roberto Bolaño, who is now having his "moment," getting his works published here.

NK: Very much so, in the wake of the translation of *The Savage Detectives*.

BG: Bolaño died in 2003. I didn't know him and this guy writes and says Roberto was a big fan of your work, he read all your stuff when it came out, especially when he was living in Spain, have you read any of his work? This was before his main works had been translated. I think I'd read a short story of his that came out here. So that was nice to know.

I was told a story once. A woman was on a train and it turned out that the guy she was on the train with was Thomas Pynchon, and she said, you're a writer, I'm friends with Barry Gifford, do you know his work? And apparently he said, oh yes, he's a good writer, but I think perhaps he publishes too much. I don't know if that is a true story, but in any event I admire his work too.

It's always nice to know that intelligent writers and readers from other cultures are following your work. You can be halfway across the world, just as you are now. I mean, I write in English, you speak English, but you speak Australian. I speak American, we know the differences and understand the distinctions, I'm using my argot du milieu, the way you do. I don't even know how many of my books are translated into these languages. I think it's something like twenty-eight languages, but how are they doing this in Czech or Rumanian? I mean, you write from a particular place and a particular time. Boy, what a struggle that must be for the translators. So you're only as good as your translator in these various countries, especially if so much of the dialogue is in dialect difficult even for American readers to parse.

NK: Are you in touch with your translators in these places, do they seek you out for advice?

BG: The only other language that I can read fairly well is French, and I have a great translator there, Jean-Paul Gratias [Amazon.fr lists translators such as Clelia Cohen, for *Do the Blind Dream?*; Claire Cera for *Wyoming*; Laetitia Devaux for *The Sinaloa Story*], who's done most of my books, and now he's doing the new Sailor and Lula one. I have had other books translated there—*Wild at Heart*, for example—and they need to retranslate that book, there were some problems with the original translation. I became friends with that translator, Richard Matas. He had also translated *Port Tropique*, which he had done a fairly good job on, but *Sailor and Lula*, as it is called there, wasn't translated as well as it could have been and should be retranslated by Jean-Paul Gratias, which I think will eventually happen. It's very difficult to gauge these things, so of course translators from all sorts of countries will write me letters asking for explanations of terms and definitions of words. I do my best to answer, and of course I'm glad some of them take the time to ask me, but boy, it's a mystery: what is it in Japanese? What is it like in a language in which I have no expertise? That's a tricky one.

NK: Jim Crumley said that in the first not-so-good translation of *The Last Good Kiss* into French (as *The Drunken Dog*), a "topless bar" became "a bar without a roof."

BG: That's really great, I like that! That's a good illustration of what I'm saying. But you're really just happy that people are getting at least some of what you're saying. I remember being told in Spain that Faulkner used not to be a very popular writer there. First of all Franco wouldn't allow his books to be translated, so the translations were done in Argentina, and apparently not very well. And I'm sure Faulkner can be a bitch to translate. So he just wasn't very highly thought of because, you know, he wasn't a very good writer if that's what he was writing! It wasn't until years later, post-Franco, that the books were retranslated and Faulkner gained the recognition that he deserved.

But also there's another thing about this. Some people's writing just doesn't work in another culture and language. I know some of my books work better in one culture/language than in others. For some reason, for years I could not get the French, who already had so many of my books in translation, to publish the books of short stories. They are finally being done now. It's very difficult to get the books of short stories published anywhere. They just don't want short stories, they want novels and I think they're missing a whole lot, because I came to the short story in a formal way, and then I fell in love with it. Often my short stories are concealed in the novels, there are many stories like that. But then I started writing just short stories and novellas, which is my favourite form.

NK: Why is the novella your favorite form?

BG: It's just the right length, you can read it all in one sitting. I also love the fact that you can spend a week or a weekend with *War and Peace*, just go through it. People also love to have "beach reading," they like long books and all. I hope the Sailor and Lula stories will be published in this country in one volume, one omnibus volume. I'm lobbying for that right now.

NK: Would that be like an Everyman edition, or a Library of America edition?

BG: I would like to see all the Sailor and Lula stories and novellas put together in one volume. Short stories in the US can get some real notoriety but they're usually not best sellers. People like to sit down and have a sustained read, and I've lately fallen in love with the short story form.

NK: With both your practical-professional and analytic knowledge of US writing traditions and institutions across several decades, you would know far better than I the history of a diminishing number of magazine formats that once existed so abundantly for that short story form. They still do to some extent—the *New Yorker*, *Harpers*, the *Atlantic Monthly*—but nowhere near the same number.

BG: Right, there are very few print venues, as opposed to online, in which to publish the short story. Most of them are academic, and then there's the *New Yorker*, and that's about it. There's no longer the *Saturday Evening Post* or *Vanity Fair* or *Scribners*, and the *Atlantic Monthly* just stopped publishing stories. When I started there were so many smaller magazines that would publish short stories; this market doesn't exist now in the same way. And it was a way for people to actually make a living, writing short stories, so I can relate a little to that, and I published a lot of short stories in a lot of magazines, and a lot in Europe too. Also excerpts from novels.

NK: I always found it odd when English publishers would say that short stories are not greatly read and are hard to sell in sufficient numbers, yet you can see people in the London tube reading them on the journey from Tufnell Park to Clapham, or wherever.

BG: Well, I'm not a publisher, I don't have the answer to that. I can only write what I write and put it out there, and hope that it'll find the reading public. Some of the chapters in *Memories from a Sinking Ship* have been published as short stories but of course they're a part of the whole, there's a connecting tissue there, that's why I publish them this way now, using and revising some of the material from *The Phantom Father*, which is published as a memoir, and *Wyoming*, as I talked about earlier, and a few from other places. And then a third of it is new work. So now I've got the whole thing, the whole canvas, but they can be read as short stories as well.

NK: In a couple of interviews I have conducted with some English publishers—Pete Ayrton at Serpent's Tail Press, and François von Hurter at Bitter Lemon Press—I have floated the analogy that says if large publishers now conduct themselves on the model of Hollywood majors, with an emphasis on blockbuster titles and saturation release through the chains, do smaller/independent publishers function more like independent cinema (even allowing for the various changes and compromises that have attended that term over the last ten years or so)? What is your sense of the publishing scene in the US at the moment, from big houses to smaller, independent outfits?

BG: Publishing really changed in the 1980s when all of a sudden the big houses started thinking of themselves as movie producers or something, or being in a similar kind of entertainment business. Well, that's not the business I came into. I was fortunate to start in this country with E. P. Dutton, a very old and revered publisher, the publisher of Joseph Conrad and A. A. Milne. I published my first novel, *Landscape with Traveler*, with them, and it was a different tradition then. I was very fortunate to start in the early 1970s and it's changed a lot, I don't think there is the same view of it as there used to be.

As always, some publishers are publishing wonderful stuff, others aren't. I think a lot of good work being done is by smaller entities who have the opportunity now because so many writers have been dropped by big publishers because of lack of sales. These are so-called mid-list writers and I'm one of them, more or less, but my notoriety with the movies seems to carry over. My books sell much better in Europe than they do here. Whit Stillman, the director, lives in Paris now, and when I saw him in New York recently, he said, "You're so famous in Europe, you're only half that here, how come?"

NK: And I guess you said, "It's not of my doing!"

BG: I said, you know, you go where you are liked and you hope you eventually get the recognition in your own country.

We started off this discussion by talking about fine presses, letterpress, and taking pride in that. Well, now, so many glitches occur because of this electronic processing. People just hit the wrong button and the whole thing is messed up. It's very weird, it really is, I hate to sound like a troglodyte, a dinosaur, but it's not so very long ago that people were setting books by hand, letter by letter.

NK: Hence the phrase, "Mind your ps and qs."

BG: Yes, and I've watched them do it. I was never a fine printer myself but I've always admired these people who seriously consider the font to use, what type will best suit the material? The history of the various fonts and so forth, that has always interested me.

NK: From favorite fonts to favorite sports. I see sitting on the piano behind me a baseball bat signed by Nellie Fox, a "Louisville Slugger"; you mentioned that it's an unusually shaped bat that you received as a gift. We haven't yet discussed your long personal, lived and literary relation to sports.

BG: Nellie Fox used a "bottle bat," a bat with an unusually thick handle. I was always interested in sports. The only two things that ever really interested me in terms of thinking about a professional future were baseball and writing, that's it. They were the only things that I ever seriously considered. I played all sports growing up, got to college and played baseball and my interest continues. When I lived in Rome I would go to the A. S. Roma soccer matches, so I'm still interested in sports. I boxed, I played baseball, football, basketball, everything that you could think of, and so did two of my sons, and my daughter was a great swimmer. I think it's a very important part of life, if you can do it, if you're able-bodied, mobile, it's a great privilege. And to me it exists as a kind of meditation. Even today when I have a baseball game on television, it's really like a meditation, there are periods of quiet and calm. I think that's why I like baseball the most.

First, it's a very subtle sport, it's not for everybody. Babe Ruth, the great baseball player, once said, and he's often quoted for the first half of this statement, "Baseball is the greatest game there is." But the second part of the statement was, "but you have to have grown up with it." And that's really right, because then you can really understand it. Otherwise it's just the home run and the strikeout, just like with Australian Rules football and soccer, it would be the goal, but there are so many other subtleties, so many things that go into it, it's hard to explain. And I think that there's been such a literature built up around baseball, and boxing too.

I think those are the two sports that have a whole literature built around them, and from them, and that's a very interesting thing. And then there are certain notable exceptions like *This Sporting Life*, for example.

NK: The one Rugby League film!

BG: But it was a novel.

NK: Yes, by David Storey.

BG: And Alan Sillitoe wrote *The Loneliness of the Long Distance Runner*, so there are certainly great individual novels or films built around a sport, like *This Sporting Life*.

NK: That raises the issue of which good films can come from excellent novels related to particular sports, and also which sports can be plausibly represented on film. For example, it's hard to think of a really good film with cricket at its center, there's something "unrepresentable" about it.

BG: There was the film *Jim Thorpe: All American* (Michael Curtiz, 1951), but that was about the Olympic champion, Jim Thorpe, who was one of my great heroes as a child. Thorpe also played professional football and baseball. He was one of my great boyhood heroes, the greatest athlete in the world at the time. I even have a copy of *The Jim Thorpe Story* here, on that bookshelf.

NK: On my last visit here my friend Jim Kitses took me to a baseball game in the new stadium down there near the harbor, and I saw Barry Bonds hit two home runs. Great to see! Later I read all this stuff about drug taking in contemporary sport.

BG: So far as drug-taking in sports is concerned, all I can say is, people are always trying to get an edge, one way or another. People call it cheating but it's just like earlier in baseball where various professional teams would station a spy in the center field stands or in the scoreboard or someplace to try to steal the catcher's signs from the other team, all sorts of things like that. Recently there was a big piece about that and the Giants and the Dodgers and a very famous game in 1954.

But in any case, you're always looking for an edge in sport. The fact that drugs came along in a particular time, well, back in the 1960s amphetamines were widely and freely used, certainly, by football players and baseball players. To get footballers out there to play, they shoot them full of bute or whatever, just like a racehorse, to get them out on the field. So, the step to steroids or human growth hormones was a very natural one, it's part of our world. Then, after it's happened, because it's always this way, always after—then it has to be regulated or banned or whatever. Then the time comes. It's like when I first came out here to

San Francisco, it was right after LSD had been criminalized. It had been created as a tranquilizer but it was certainly one step beyond, so the government classified it as a narcotic, a dangerous drug.

NK: Well Kesey and others had done those experiments, some of which are touched on in Robert Stone's recent memoir, *Prime Green*.

BG: As early as the late '50s and early '60s people were experimenting with LSD in various instances, sometimes academic, like Leary at Harvard, we know all this. The point is that, when you know what animal you've got, then you have to deal with it. It's a similar thing with the use of drugs in sports, that's all, and now they're figuring out what to do with it. As for the use of human growth hormone or steroid use, in baseball and football teams, the owners of these teams aren't concerned whether this is good or bad for you, that's not their primary concern.

NK: What do you think of the practice of relocation of teams such that a New York based team, with all of that history, winds up on the West Coast? What does that do to fans?

BG: The owners don't give a shit about the fan, it's all about money. What does the word "professional" connote? It means you get paid for what you do. You have a professional sports team, well if you don't get the fans coming out, or you think you can move to an area where it's going to be more lucrative, they do it! They're all carpetbaggers, that's what's going on, there's no mystery in this.

NK: Well, you might have to follow the impact of the arrival of David Beckham into LA and US soccer, maybe the biggest thing since the moment of Pelé and Franz Beckenbauer and the New York Cosmos.

BG: Well, when these guys are past it they come to America to collect! I've never followed soccer in the States but it should be bigger here than it is. When I was growing up, kids didn't play soccer in the US. There were very, very few teams and now, in the last thirty years, kids growing up in the suburban culture play soccer, because there is room for it.

NK: In Australia there was a moment at which soccer was thought less likely to lead to a serious injury, compared with other winter sports such as AFL, Rugby Union and Rugby League, and so there was a kind of mothers' advocacy group for soccer.

BG: It's funny, when I first went to London I played some cricket, I was asked to come by, as a baseball player, and I got the hang of it, and I enjoyed that a little bit. And then I did a term at Kings College in Cambridge, and I played on the American soccer team there. In fact our goalkeeper was Gene Siskel, of Siskel-Ebert, the TV movie critics. And I had a good time doing that but I didn't really know how to play soccer so I related it to hockey, and that's how I was able to think of it, visualise it and learn what to do. It was kind of like Babe Ruth saying you had to have grown up with it. I couldn't "handle" the ball, but I had to figure out what I could do so that I could contribute in some way. I had a good slapshot in ice hockey, even though I wasn't a good skater. So you adapt, you figure out what you can contribute, and that's interesting to me, figuring out what your value can be, how you can make the best use of your skills, that sort of stuff.

But the rugby guys, boy, I still think that's the roughest game there is. I played a little in England. I was a running back and a quarterback in American football, but in rugby there isn't any blocking! Boy, my admiration goes out to those guys, they're tough. The University of California at Berkeley has dominated collegiate level rugby in America for years.

NK: Do you ever find it odd as you move between your fiction writing, done alone, apart from others, as you described your writing regimen earlier, and your movie writing which is collaborative and brings you into a much more public, heightened celebrity culture, not that literary culture doesn't have its version of that as well.

BG: I don't really court celebrity and in the movie business it's really hard to avoid. Years ago I remember a producer saying, it's time you hired a publicist, you're doing work for Coppola, you've got a couple of books that have done very well, you're living with a famous Italian movie star, you've got to get a publicist. And I said, "Why? You already know everything!" I thought it was an unseemly suggestion, but you walk a tightrope here, because you need to have a certain amount of publicity in order to have people pay attention to your work. For instance, submitting to interviews. Why are we sitting here doing this? Is it because people are really interested in how I write, what I write and what's in my head or whatever? I guess people want to know what I'm thinking, and I should be properly flattered, but the truth is in the work. It's all there, as B. Traven said.

NK: It's good to see your essay on him open your recent collection, *The Cavalry Charges*.

BG: Now, he had an agenda, a reason for hiding or disguising himself, but he was also thirsting for attention and that showed in how he lived his life in Mexico City. Anyway it's a really double-edged sword. You have to have a certain amount of exposure. But I'm a bit of a reluctant dragon. I guess I have been for a long time, for forever. I could have done a lot more but I've sort of discouraged it. I'm hopeful that the work will survive and that some of it will resonate, entertain and be appreciated, and my efforts haven't been a waste of time and energy.

NOEL KING teaches in the Department of Media at Macquarie University, Sydney, Australia. One current research interest of his concerns "Cultures of Independence": a study of small and/or independent publishers in Australia, the UK, and the USA. His (relatively recent) interviews with the publishers at Fremantle Arts Centre Press, Scribe Press, Steerforth Press, Bitter Lemon Press, and Serpent's Tail Press have appeared in *Westerly*, *Metro*, *Heat*, and *Critical Quarterly*, respectively. He also has an ongoing study of contemporary international crime fiction (in English) involving both English language works and translated works, a study of writers, publishers, and critics in the UK and the US.

ABOUT BARRY GIFFORD

The author of more than forty published works of fiction, nonfiction, and poetry, which have been translated into twenty-eight languages, BARRY GIFFORD writes distinctly American stories for millions of readers around the globe. He is the literary heir of Conrad, of Hemingway, of Algren and Camus, exposing the underbelly of the American Dream in ever surprising twists and turns. His novel *Wild at Heart* was made into a film by David Lynch, which won the Palme d'Or at the Cannes Film Festival, and his novel *Perdita Durango* was made into a feature film by Alex de la Iglesia. He cowrote, with David Lynch, the film *Lost Highway*, and with Matt Dillon, the film *City of Ghosts*. Gifford has received awards from PEN, the National Endowment for the Arts, the American Library Association, the Writers Guild of America, and the Premio Brancati in Italy. For more information, visit www.BarryGifford.com.